Things that annoy me by Ruby Brady

Kay Carlton

Dedication

For my own little "Ruby"

who always makes me laugh

August 10th 2017

MY NEW JOURNAL

OMG that is SO annoying!!

So, I'm writing this because I just got told, AGAIN, to "get off that bloody phone and stop looking at pointless crap on YouTube" - my Mum totally doesn't get it. It's alright when she wants to be on Facebook being all stupid with her mates, making jokes about wine o'clock and how hard it is being a parent, but when I want to talk with MY friends there are apparently more IMPORTANT things I should be doing and it's not good for my brain to be on the phone ALL the time... blah blah blah.....

She says I should be reading more books or I will be "struggling at school." I'm doing fine at school - and school is really boring and totally useless anyway. I'm MOST annoyed because I wasn't even ON YouTube at the time. I hadn't even finished doing my streaks and I was totally in the middle of a really important snapchat with Izzy about Rob (her future boyfriend - she hopes).

Honestly, it REALLY, REALLY annoys me.

Other stuff that annoys me .....

- • When Mum says "swanky"

- • When Mum asks me if I've got any homework (I don't know why... it just annoys me)

- • When Mum asks me if I've got homework again (because she was reading the WhatsApp messages from "The Gang" and not listening to me the first time)

- • The fact that she calls her mates "The Gang" (so annoying)

- • When Mum TRIES to use modern words (soooo embarrassing)

- • When she puts pictures of me on Instagram, without even asking!

- • When Mum and Uncle David make comments about "Insta-face", "Gram-chat" and "Snap-book" .. they think it's SOOOO funny (which it isn't). It's just CRINGE!!!!

So anyway, I'm Ruby Brady and I'm nearly 13 - I will be 13 in October and I'm going into year 8 at Springleaf Comprehensive School. Actually, I'm lucky that I'm even called Ruby ... my Mum is like this frustrated hippy and she thought it would be cool to give me a "different" name. She wanted to call me Moonbeam … Seriously!!! Moonbeam!!   Yeah. It's soooooooooo embarrassing!!!!! Fortunately Grandma told her not to be 'so bloody ridiculous' and she actually listened (for once). Mum's name is Janice which she hates!! She said it's a terrible name and Grandma really could have come up with something more modern - so she calls herself Jaz instead. She thinks it sounds cooler. Whatever.

Mum always said if she was born earlier she'd totally have been a proper hippy - all bare feet and flowers in her hair. It's something to do with San Francisco and some song. She's like backpacked ALL over the world, which I actually think is quite cool, but I don't tell HER that.

She doesn't like having an ordinary boring job - she always has some new idea of something to do or some latest trend she is following - it's exhausting. At the moment she is apparently on a "personal development journey" and experiencing the beginning of a "spiritual awakening" whatever that is! From what I can see it just involves buying lots of books and these stupid crystals and putting inspirational quotes on Facebook all the time and not much else. Well apart from moaning at me that is!!

If it was up to her she'd probably be covered in tattoos living in a yurt on a beach somewhere, poncing around being all "spiritual" and homeschooling me. The only reason she doesn't is:

1) She has to earn a living in order to pay for all the make-up and clothes that I'm always asking for … (that's what she says - that's annoying!)

and

b) Grandma would probably tell her not to be so bloody ridiculous.

She already tried being a teacher once, a very long time ago, and she didn't like it, so the homeschooling part would be a total disaster!! And whatever other rubbish she believes, she's always saying that a good education is really important.

I'm quite glad really, as I like living here and I don't want to live in a yurt or a tiny eco-house or be a nomad living off of the land. I like going to school the same as NORMAL people and I like my life.

And actually it IS a pretty normal life … there's me, my Mum, my stepdad Neville and the idiot dog. We did have a hamster for a while but our family isn't very lucky with hamsters. Turns out Neville bought a dead one anyway. Well to be entirely truthful, the hamster wasn't actually dead when he bought it. He bought it for me as a surprise and the lady offered to keep it for us until we got back from our holiday. It died before we came back, so she bought a replacement one for us because she felt so guilty about selling us a rubbish pet. But we always joke about the time Neville bought me a dead hamster … ha ha. It was a pretty boring pet to be honest and it kept escaping so in the end we sold it when we got the dog. Mum said the hamster was only a "starter pet" to see how I got on looking after it. TBH it was a really stinky thing so I didn't miss it much. My friend Charlotte's mum says that you only buy hamsters in order to "teach children about death." Mum said that when she was small Grandpa buried her hamster alive so I guess I was lucky. She said she was convinced it was hibernating 'cos it said so in her book, so after a bit of tutting from Grandpa and lots of tears from Mum, Grandpa dug it up again. It was DEFINITELY dead by then. Grandma and Grandpa don't like pets. Grandma once left my Auntie's Giant African Snail in the boot of her car in winter because she forgot about it and it froze to death. Auntie Sophie was really young at the time and she was devastated but one of Mum's Australian mates was visiting and he suggested they should "stick the little mongrel by the radiator', said he'd probably 'thaw out like a champ." They tried that but the house stank of rotting snail according to Mum and he was still dead at the end of it. The Australian bloke apparently said that was "Fair Dinkum" but I don't know what that means.

So far we haven't had a problem with the dog - apart from the dog being an Idiot. I wanted a dog for ages and I thought I might be a vet when I'm older but when I told Grandma she said that vets spend all day doing "unspeakable things to the backsides of pigs and cows", so I decided working for The Dog's Trust would be a much better plan. That's the sort of thing that Grandma says. Auntie Sophie wanted to be a GP when she was young but Grandma told her she'd have to chop up dead bodies. Auntie Sophie is a bit squeamish so now she's an accountant instead. Grandma is always chopping stuff up - she doesn't care, she seems to enjoy it. Her dad was a butcher so she can take chickens apart or cut fishes heads off and it doesn't make her feel icky AT ALL!! She will eat anything too - kidneys, liver, snails - urggghghh!. Grandpa says he's scared of being in a plane crash where him and Grandma end up on a desert island, as he knows that Grandma will eat him. Grandma always just smiles and says that Grandpa is probably right. Grandma thinks that Grandpa only asked her out on a second date because after they got back from the first one, her dad made Grandpa the biggest bacon sandwich he'd ever seen in his life!

So anyway - this journal. It was Mum's idea as she JUST came back from Bali - she'd gone on some retreat to "get in touch with her true authentic self and find her deep soul purpose" or some such crap. She came back all calm and zen and was all green juice and yoga and meditation for about 4 days. She kept on about compassion and gratitude and patience. That lasted about 5 minutes before she started nagging me about the state of my room, wearing too much make-up and watching pointless shit on YouTube again.... She said they spent lot of time in Bali journaling and that it's really valuable to "understand your feelings" and "get your emotions out of your body and onto the page."

What. EVER!!

Still …. she brought me this really pretty journal back as a gift - it has a really colourful cover and says "Dream Big" on the front. I thought I might start writing in it and record a bit of my life ... so here it is …

Gotta go - dinner's ready and me and Mum are bingeing old episodes of Gilmore Girls on Netflix so we will hopefully get a couple in before bed.

August 12th

OMG - I'm soooooooooo tired. Mum's friends were round last night for "girls night."   They are all old so I don't get the "girl" part - they are all 40 odd and some are even 50!! Seriously. SAD.

They were out in the garden for ages getting really red in the sunshine and taking loads of pictures of each other. Then they decided to come indoors later and get comfy. Neville locked himself in the other room and played on the Xbox as they were all shrieking really loudly in the lounge and keeping me awake. I don't know what they talk about all the time but there are always a MILLION empty bottles in the morning. Seems to me they sit round drinking a ton of Prosecco and moaning that they can't lose weight. Then they eat loads of crisps or sweets or whatever there is in the cupboard.

Honestly, even I can see that doesn't make sense!! I thought adults had stuff figured out.

Mum looked terrible this morning and was pretending not to have a hangover - but she's completely rubbish at acting. She looks better now I'm back from seeing everyone at the park and is busy making a healthy salad for dinner and rattling on about veganism. She had vegan food the whole time she was in Bali and said it was wonderful. I'm sure it helped that a special chef made all the food. Strangely the bacon I wanted to have on my bagel has disappeared. She said Neville must have eaten it but it was there this morning and he's not even home from work yet. She totally had a hangover bacon sandwich and isn't admitting it. Great start to being a vegan. That's gonna last. NOT.

Just heard a massive crash - the idiot dog is standing in the middle of the lounge with a cat flap round her middle. The back door has a cat flap in it so we trained the dog to go through it when she was a new puppy. It WAS working fine, but the dog is a git and is now too FAT for the cat flap. She is a sausage obsessed lunatic and would eat all day if we let her. And not just sausages - chicken, bacon, cheese, salmon - anything apart from dog food. She ignores that all day hoping something better will come along. She even eats tin foil and poo sometimes - it's disgusting. She doesn't answer to her own name but she does answer to either "chicken" or "bacon" - I think we should change her name. No one uses her proper name anyway. Mum calls her "The Idiot" and Neville calls her "The Pig". It's no wonder she doesn't respond - she's probably got no idea what she's really called. Mum also calls her Thickie the Wonder Dog - it's some joke connected to a TV programme about a horse from when she was young - like a MILLION years ago.

Actually, I don't mind old programmes - Mum and Neville got me to watch Faulty Towers, Vicar of Dibley, Black Adder and a bunch of other really funny ones. We just finished watching Absolutely Fabulous - I think Mum likes it because she thinks her and her mates are a bit like Edina and Patsy and I'm a bit like Saffie - except I'm not as boring and my clothes are way nicer! But I know what she meant, especially the part where they are always drunk and falling out of taxis. Not that Mum has fallen out of a taxi … well she probably has, I just haven't seen it happen.

Right now she's standing in the middle of the room looking gormless. Not Mum. The Dog.

Me and Mum try to wrestle her out of the cat flap but it's no good - it's wedged round her belly. Neville will have to sort it out when he gets in. The dog actually behaves for him.

I've just been getting ready for bed. Mum keeps shouting up the stairs that it's getting late. I know what time it is for goodness sake. I'm trying to put my hair into plaits so it's curly in the morning and Mum is moaning that it's taking too long. She doesn't get that it's important that it looks right. The same as she doesn't get that eyebrows are really, REALLY important. She keeps saying they look a bit too "obvious" - what does that even mean??? Of course they are obvious … they are eyebrows, they take up a big chunk of your face!!! Then she tried to be cool and asked if they are "on fleek" or "peng". So embarrassing. Turned out she'd seen someone say it on Facebook and looked it up in The Urban Dictionary.

Honestly. Parents.

PS: Neville got the cat flap off of the dog. He said that even though the dog is a "f**king moron" she's more intelligent than most of the people he had to deal with at work today.

August 14th

Mum has been going on about all sorts of stuff since she came back from Bali. Right now she is all about "decluttering" and getting rid of anything that doesn't bring her "joy". It's from yet another self-help book by a Japanese woman about tidying up and how your life will change if you get rid of anything that isn't joyful. She's been in the kitchen all day emptying the contents of the cupboards and throwing stuff away. Neville is furious - he's trying to fish various pans and roasting tins out of the bin and ranting that they might not spark joy but it's pretty f**king impossible to cook the f**king dinner without any f**king pots and pans.

She's been decluttering things all day and frankly the mood her and Neville are both in has got absolutely nothing to do with joy!! I happened to mention this and she said that neither me or Neville will understand until we read the book and find out what the "Kon Marie method" actually is. Neville said, "Alright then let's see what this is all about" and stomped off to the toilet with the book.

He came back a bit later laughing his head off saying, "Well I've heard everything now Jaz ... apparently I should be folding my socks a certain way to keep them 'happy' in the chest of drawers ... hahahaha .... apparently they have a very difficult life and when they are not on our manky, stinking feet we should be making life comfortable for them ..... Happy f**king socks?? I've heard some crap in my time but really, who are the sh***ing idiots that believe this tripe?"

I started to giggle along with him and told her it did sound a bit ridiculous. Neville turned to me and said, "What do you reckon

Ruby, between my fungal foot infections and my bunion I bet my socks have a right old time of it."

Urghhghgh - why did he have to tell me that?? Disgusting. Put me right off my wagon wheel.

August 19th

OMG - why is it a problem for me to be on my phone!!!!! Mum just constantly has a go about it!! And Neville is just as bad when he's actually here. It's not like Mum and Neville are even talking to me tonight! Honestly - so annoying. Mum is on Facebook and Neville is wearing stupid headphones and playing some stupid Xbox game, and looking STUPID. Facebook is rubbish - only REALLY OLD people think it's good. Mum tries to do a bit of Instagram - mostly putting embarrassing pictures of me on there without even asking .... so CRINGE! And neither of them understand Snapchat AT ALL! They only like Facebook because that is kind of how they met - apparently. They spent ages sending each other stupid messages and making comments on each other's pictures that they said were really funny, but they probably weren't. That was years ago anyway. These days Neville just posts load of stupid jokes (that aren't funny) and rants about stuff. Mum posts a bunch of spiritual crap and deep and meaningful quotes - or just stalks people whose posts annoy her and then rants about them. Both of them just annoy me!

Mum's been on FaceTime for about an hour with Auntie Eleanor - she is Mum's older sister. She lives in Geneva and she has a really important job that is something to do with the Government and Economics and Climate Change stuff.

We are going to get a bigger flap fitted in the back door. Also the dog needs to go on a diet.

August 20th

Mum is having a loud rant to Neville about someone called Debbie. She lives in our town and Mum sort of knows her... well 'sort of' meaning they occasionally comment on each other's Facebook posts, but they aren't really friends. Debbie apparently has three kids that are always ill and Debbie seems to have to share every aspect of their illnesses with the whole world. God how boring! Who cares. Well, Mum does because it annoys her. To be fair I think it would annoy me too. I just heard her say, "Neville - look at this - the middle one has got some sort of weird thing on her thigh.. and there's a photo of it and she's asking if people know what it is." Neville replied, "Silly f**king cow, why doesn't she go to the doctors like a normal person?? Does she think 'Barry down the pub' will miraculously diagnose it???"

They are both getting quite annoyed - I was pretty tempted to tell them "to get off the bloody phone" but I'd probably get in trouble. Just shows what hypocrites the pair of them are!!

Now Mum is complaining about the Applebys again. The Applebys are this perfect family with twins. Their Facebook page is full of family days out and everything is hash tagged - #familyqualitytime and #makingmemories. Mrs Appleby is what Mum calls "one of those sickeningly perfect Pinterest Mums" who is always making absolutely everything from scratch and doing crafting projects with

13

the twins. Since it's a Sunday Mr Appleby is in lots of the pictures too, there are hundreds of them out collecting sloes and blackberries from the hedgerows, carrying little matching baskets and making homemade crumble. Neville shouted, "Hashtag making f**king memories? Hashtag making me sick more like."

I said I thought it was nice that they were having a lovely family day together and that we never do stuff like that. Neville said, "Well if you want to do something we can all go down to the pub and have a family drink together." Go to the pub. Typical. That's his answer to everything. In the end I decided that it was better than nothing and said yes we should go.

Neville ruined it when we got there by turning round to Mum and saying, "What do you fancy for a bever-ar-gini Jaz" in a really loud voice. It was so embarrassing. Chloe's WHOLE family were in there having Sunday lunch!! Utterly cringe!

August 21st

Mum has been on the phone to Margaret for hours and hours - she's Mum's really old friend - old like she's known her for ever but she's also OLD. They used to travel together all the time before I was born and before Neville came along. Whenever they get together they talk rubbish for hours about the old days and drink loads of wine and end up being all embarrassing and screeching with laughter. Margaret has just moved further away so they don't get to see each other so often. Sounds like there's another drama with Margaret's cats!! There's always a drama - they are like killing machines - they always bring in tons of half dead mice and other animals in the house and leave bits of intestines everywhere. Sometimes Margaret

treads in them when she gets out of bed - yuk! I
The Midsummer Murders but with various diffe
The cats have posh names that I can't remembe
them Ronnie & Reggie. Apparently they were t
that used to live in London and murdered peopl

Not much h
no real dr
few da

I seriously don't like cats - I don't like that they kill mice and birds
and stuff. The idiot dog doesn't even do that - the worst thing she
does in roll in poo and empty the bins all the time.

Speaking of rolling in poo - Neville has just returned from a walk
and the Idiot STINKS - OMG - it's disgusting!!!!! Mum had finally
stopped talking to Margaret about a half dead mouse that had
chewed through her best John Lewis curtains, so she ran upstairs
when Neville shouted for her. Apparently cleaning the Idiot was a 2
person job. She is in the bath and they are covering her in ketchup
(because Mum's mate Suzie said it neutralises the smell). I poked
my head round the door on the way to my room and the two of them
were wrestling with the idiot and there was ketchup all over the
walls, the bath and the ceiling …. it looked like an ACTUAL murder
scene!!!

Also the weird thing on Debbie's daughter's leg has started to
multiply - there is a horrible photo of a lot of oozing lumps and
bumps that she's scratched. Urghhgh! There are loads of people still
telling her that she should get off Facebook and take the child to the
doctors, or ring the NHS helpline, but she isn't listening.

August 24th

s been going on... been so busy with all my friends and
amas - AMAZINGLY! The weather's been lovely the last
ys so we've had lots of sunny evenings outside.

Mum has an old friend staying from when she lived in Australia -
I've hardly seen her, they've been out and about all the time in the
day and drinking lots of wine in the garden in the evening and telling
stories about all the crazy nights out they used to have. Neville
wasn't there, so he isn't really interested. He has just been spending
waaaay more time on the Xbox and letting them get on with it. It's
fine with me because she hasn't moaned ONCE about me being on
the phone - total miracle!!

It's a bit weird - whenever Mum is with her old friends and they are
talking about someone or something - Mum leaps up and starts
rummaging through all these old photo albums and then they sit and
look through them laughing and hugging and saying stuff like "that
was a hell of a night" or "remember the comedy Bavarian." [I don't
know what a Bavarian is...] Honestly though, why would you bother
with all those prints? You can just look these people up on
Instagram!! It's weird the obsession old people have with photo
albums. Grandma is the same she has TONS of them!! Mind you it
was quite cool when she showed me these old creased brown photos
that were of my great, great, Grandpa in his war uniform! Made me
think a bit … what if Instagram just disappears? We might not be
able to do that in the future .. all the pictures might just be lost
somewhere … That IS weird.

Debbie's other children are now all scratching having sat out in the
sunshine last night and been bitten by midges. The Applebys on the
other hand don't have a single bite despite having lots of family
picnics, long days out at inflatable water parks, masses of bike rides
and hours and hours in the enormous paddling pool and slide thing

that they've put in the garden. It's massive!! It's bigger than the bouncy castle I had for a party when I was 7!!

Neville seems particularly annoyed by the photos of Mr Appleby learning to waterski and keeps muttering things like "hashtag fun in the water" and "hashtag I'm a smug twat."

Mum just said, "Well he can certainly pull off a wetsuit - that's pretty unusual in a bloke over 40." I thought that was a bit strange - surely you need to be able to pull off the wetsuit when you get out of the water, however old you are.

August 25th

Today was rubbish - we had to go shopping for school stuff - that always puts Mum in a right mood. There are certain things we can only get from this one special shop because they have the school crest on and they cost three times the price of the same thing without the crest from M&S or Next. Last year she insisted on getting me plain PE shirts, even though I told her it was a waste of time and that she'd have to take them back and get the ones with the crest on but she wouldn't listen. Sure enough the PE teacher told me off and gave me a warning and we had to go and buy the right ones.

We had a row about shoes too. The ones she wanted to get me are like old women's shoes. She keeps saying it doesn't matter because they are "only school shoes and no one will notice." Of course they will notice!! I managed to convince her to get the ones that I wanted by pretending all the other ones didn't fit right and would end up giving me blisters.

Hated thinking about school today. I want summer to keep going on for a few more weeks. Neville is the only person that is happy for summer to end - it's because he keeps burning his bald head.

August 27th

Another Sunday evening and another Appleby rant! The Applebys have been camping all weekend and are all wearing matching T-shirts that say "Appleby Adventures." There's also now an Appleby Adventures Facebook page to show all their holiday adventures. The page has a logo at the top that is the same as the T-shirts and features 2 big red apples and 2 little red apples - they all have legs and arms and smiley faces!! I actually think it's cute but you can imagine Neville's reaction!

The camping looked fun - in proper tents in the middle of nowhere - they were fishing and building dens and all sorts of stuff. I said to Mum and Neville that we should do that sometime. They said they'd think about it. Not getting too excited they hardly ever keep their promises.

September 1st

Been hanging out at the park all day with Em, Izzy and some of the boys. There were a few of them there today as everyone is pretty much back from their holidays. James A and James B were there and Jack and Connor. Harry was there too - or "pointless boyfriend" as we call him. Neville named him that, it's from when we were in Junior School and he was my boyfriend. We supposedly "went out" for like 2 whole terms - quite a long time for Juniors really. Well I say that we went out - we obviously didn't actuallyGO OUT anywhere. In fact, we didn't really even speak to each other, it was just generally accepted that he was my boyfriend. Neville said if all romantic relationships involved you never having to do anything with the other person or even having to communicate with them, life would be a lot simpler.

Today was so much fun - we played dodgeball, took a ton of selfies and then went to town for ice-creams. We have to go back to school in 4 days!!!! This has been the BEST summer - I don't want it to end.

September 3rd

We FaceTimed Uncle John today and all my American cousins. Uncle John has lived in America for years but we haven't visited since I was a little baby. It's mainly because Mum has this huge list of places she wants to go to and she is working her way through it. America is NOT on the list. I always wanted to go to Disney but Mum says it's a load of commercialised nonsense and not worth paying good money for.

So there's my cousin Jamie who is a bit older than me and she is super cool. She has recently turned into "a bit of a goth" according to Grandma - I don't think wearing black and dip-dying your hair really makes you a goth but WHATEVER! There are also my little boy cousins as well. Uncle John is married to Emmy-Lou these days and they have Chad & Brad the twins. Emmy-Lou is much younger than Uncle John and she has lots of guns. She even has a pink gun. Usually when we FaceTime, Chad and Brad are just fighting in the background. Mum says Uncle John never got the hang of political correctness (whatever that is) and is a bit of a racist. He doesn't mind people calling him a racist - in fact he seems to find it quite funny and says stuff deliberately to wind Mum and Auntie Eleanor up. He says stuff like "calling someone a Paki doesn't make me racist." They both get really angry about it but he just laughs. On FaceTime he was telling this story about going out for dinner and said, "It was hilarious actually, it was an Indian restaurant so I called the waiter Mowgli for the entire meal." Then he just laughed his head off about it for ages. Mum said he will get himself beaten up one of these days and that it's dangerous to be rude to people in restaurants because they can mess with your food. Uncle John said he was actually pretty sick for most of the next day. So Neville replied, "Yeah that guy totally pissed in your dinner." Ughghh! Horrible.

Uncle John was trying to tell us about their plans to come to England for Christmas but Chad punched Brad in the face so we had to cut the FaceTime short.

September 5th

Ughh! School. Why can't I still be on holiday ?????????????????????????????

Good news though - there is a new boy in 8KC. FIT!!

September 6th

Mum has a really, really big hangover AGAIN - her and all the gang were out last night celebrating the fact the summer holidays are over. Honestly! Parents are supposed to enjoy spending time with us! They go on and on about how much they will miss us on Facebook (so they look like decent loving parents) then go out to celebrate the fact we aren't around all day. Nice!

I asked Mum why there's a massive pile of mints, four spoons, a salt and pepper pot and about 30 sachets of sugar on the counter in the kitchen. Apparently Jane stole them from the restaurant last night and put them in Mum's handbag when she wasn't looking. Mum says Jane doesn't look like the sort of person that would steal things but she can't help herself (or Helen always dares her to do it) so she's always taking stuff. She tried to steal a traffic cone outside the pub last night apparently, but got told off by a security guard. They are massive - it's not like she could have hidden it under her dress! She did get two candle holders from the bar though. Neville reckons they have CCTV so they will probably have seen her. There's a massive candelabra in Lizzie's house that Jane stole from a work Christmas party one year. She keeps it at Lizzie's house because they have a really big table that it looks good on.

I thought stealing was bad, but Mum and Neville were sniggering about the traffic cone for ages saying it's only a bit of fun. Whenever the teenagers in the town do stuff like that we don't hear the end of it from Neville. They are "layabouts" and "herberts" and "lazy f**king Oiks" but it's alright if it's Jane doing it. I don't get the pair of them sometimes.

September 7th

Mum has resurrected the yoga again this week. She is sitting downstairs with some incense burning and some crap music on that "reminds her of Bali" .. she's been back for 4 whole weeks .. why isn't she over it yet? She keeps rattling on about it being a special spiritual place and how it had a deep profound effect on her soul. I'm bored of it. I tried to show her a James Charles make-up video that was really cool but I could tell she wasn't really concentrating.

Something really funny happened at lunch break today, I got a pea stuck up my nose, I was being stupid sticking it in my nose and pulling faces then I snorted and laughed at the same time and it went UP my nostril and got stuck. I had to go to Matron who removed it with some tweezers, it was so hilariously embarrassing and me Em and Izzy were still laughing about it in science so we got told off by Mr Piggott. He's always telling people off he's sooooo miserable. And Katie W was crying AGAIN and he didn't know what to do. He just stood there like a plum being useless!!!! He's so annoying. We ALL think he looks like exactly like a potato. Mum wasn't happy when I told her that as she had to go to parents evening the next week. She said she tried really hard to listen to what he was saying, but couldn't concentrate because she was just thinking about potatoes the WHOLE time. And then she told me a boring story about her friend that used to work for a man that looked like a squirrel.

Neville came home from work in a really bad mood, muttering something about "sh**ting idiots".

Neville works at this place where they deliver loads of food to pubs and hotels and stuff all over the country. So this man at work managed to get frostbite in his earlobes because he went into a massive freezer without a balaclava on (which is against the rules, they HAVE to wear them). He'd got these big discs put in his earlobes that made holes the size of tennis balls, so when he got really cold the thin bits of his ears froze solid!! Turns out he'll have to have them chopped off. Yuk. Mum starting banging on about these practices being culturally significant within certain African Tribes (the big round ear piercing part not the going in the freezer part) and that it's disrespectful for "some idiot from Essex" to mimic this in the name of fashion. Neville just called him "dangerously stupid" and muttered something I didn't really understand about natural selection.

September 10th

Mum is supposed to be working on a bunch of logos for a local restaurant but she keeps getting distracted by Facebook. Two of Debbie's children have got nits again for the 4th time in 2 weeks. There are photos of all the kids covered in nit shampoo. I used to hate when that happened when I was smaller - yuk. Makes me feel itchy just talking about it. All the mums seem to be pitching in and sharing their opinions on different types of shampoo and combs, and complaining about the parents that "can't be bothered to sort their children's hair out properly." Don't any of them have actual jobs? They seem to spend hours commenting on boring Facebook posts.

Neville was just commenting that Debbie's children had gone a whole couple of weeks without a story about vomiting on Facebook when Mum said, "Oh God one of them has just thrown up from the smell of the nit shampoo - it's all over the bathroom rug apparently."

I asked Mum what time we would be having dinner but she said she was far too busy working on her logo ideas to get food ready for everyone. Neville said, "Looks more like you are on Facebook to me Jaz." She said, "Oh piss off Neville" and "Get yourself a bit of toast Ruby, we'll sort something out later." I went off to do a group FaceTime with Izzy and Em about the fact that my Mother hardly ever remembers that I need dinner at all, never mind something actually nutritious.

Izzy is still really keen on Rob but he doesn't really seem interested in her. Or any of the other girls to be honest. We've decided he might be gay.

"We'll sort something out later" turned out to be Mum sending Neville down the chip shop so actually that turned out alright. Mum said she didn't want anything as it was all greasy and unhealthy and she'd make herself a salad. She DID make a salad, but then she took half of Neville's chips which put him in a really bad mood, so he spent the rest of the night on the Xbox.

I had a battered sausage which would have been great, except for the fact the Idiot sat there staring at me the whole time I ate it. She kept looking really sad as if no one ever feeds her so I had to give in and let her have a tiny bit.

Sept 16th

A man came round to the house yesterday to fit a big dog flap for the Idiot because she's too fat. Even though this is still a hole in the SAME door, the dog is too stupid to figure out she can go through it, just like she's been doing for the last 2 years. She just kept sticking her head through it and looking confused. We had to actually OPEN the back door to let her in and out - RIDICULOUS. Neville said, "Just shove her through and she'll get the hang of it" and demonstrated by grabbing her, pointing her in the direction of the dog flap and pushing her backside really hard. She didn't want to come back in at first, but as soon as I sat the other side of the door holding a big piece of cheddar she figured it out pretty quickly.

Mum had friends over again and she told them about the new dog flap, very loudly!!! It's only just gone lunch time and all her friends are already on the Prosecco and rambling on about how their jeans don't fit anymore, whilst eating a full English breakfast cooked up by Neville. I decided to go out and meet Izzy to form our plan about her and Rob.

I've just come home and Mum's friends are STILL there!! They've been on the wine for hours (of course) and are getting louder and louder and starting to loll on the sofa and spill stuff. I just got some biscuits and left. The idiot was upstairs on my bed and as I went over to stroke her I stepped in something wet. She had brought in a squashed slug from the garden!!! UGHHH.

Apparently Mum's friend Katie is worried that the new dog flap is a total security risk. She thinks midget burglars could get in and rob us blind. There are lots of things that happen in our town but seeing loads of midgets in the streets acting suspiciously isn't one of them. I agree with Mum - what are the chances of someone fitting through the dog flap??

September 17th

We went out for a Sunday roast at the pub. Mum and Neville both wanted some wine so we left the car in town and walked all the way home. When we got home Neville remembered the front door keys were still in the car. Him and Mum started to argue about him being a "useless twat". They were so busy arguing they didn't notice me climb on the bin and jump over the fence. Then I went round the back of the house and crawled in through the dog flap to open the house from the inside. I guess Katie was right - it wouldn't be that hard to rob us. Still …. I was impressed by my quick thinking and it saved Neville a long walk back to the car so he was quite pleased.

Even though they'd had loads of drinks at lunch time they decided to sit in the garden and drink more wine. Drinking at lunchtime doesn't work for either of them - they laugh and joke and mess around but then they usually end up shouting at each other later or they both fall asleep on the sofa at about 5 o'clock.

Luckily today was a falling asleep day. I FaceTimed Em for a chat and then started to film them both lolling about with their mouths wide open for a laugh!!! Suddenly Neville did a massive snore and woke himself up, looking a bit shocked - it was sooooooooooo hard not to giggle - I made it look like I was playing on the phone and wandered out of the room quickly while I still had a sort of straight face. Hilarious!

No idea if they got up later and went to bed or if they slept there all night. Don't really care to be honest.

September 18th

Ha - neither of them looked so hot this morning, there was lots of complaining about Monday mornings and having to deal with "shit" at work. Mum was supposed to sort me out a packed lunch for today and forgot. There is nothing in the house — I will have to get something disgusting from the canteen!! Also I JUST realised I don't have a clean PE kit. Urgghh! ... I will have to wear my stinking polo shirt AGAIN. What is wrong with my mother?????? Can't she occasionally pick the stuff up off of my floor and put it in the washing machine?? It's not too much to ask. India's Mum is always super organised.

I said that to Mum, but she just lost her temper and said, "Yes and I'd be organised too if didn't have to actually go to work and had a full time cleaner, gardener, au pair and someone to do all the ironing." Then she took two headache tablets and sprayed my PE top with a load of Febreze.

After all that I got to school and realised that I'd left the PE kit at home anyway - Mum moaned a lot but said she'd drive to school and drop it off. It's not like it's far, I don't see what the big deal is. She said when she was young if she forgot something it was tough and she'd just have to face a detention. She reckons kids today are totally wrapped in cotton wool and their parents are way too soft on them. What rubbish! She's not that soft on me... although she does always bring stuff to school that I've forgotten even if she does moan about it.

She'd cheered up a bit by the time I got home from school mainly because Bridget called and said let's all pop to the wine bar later and Mum laughed and starting saying something about the "hair of the dog."

In fairness the dog could do with having her hair sorted out. She looks ridiculous! Neville said he wasn't prepared to pay "an f**king fortune" for someone to give the dog a haircut and a bath, so he got some clippers from Amazon and did it himself. She looked pretty lopsided and seemed to have the sort of dodgy-looking haircut that people had when Mum and Neville were young.

Neville just laughed and said, "I seem to have made her look a bit Jimmy Saville" and Mum told him never to mention that name as it makes her feel physically sick. I have no idea who they were talking about but Mum said, "It's a good job I never posted my letter to Jim'll Fix It in the end that's all I can say" and Neville said, "They should just round up every single TV presenter from the 70s and that would be an end to it." Honestly I really have no clue what they are on about most of the time.

Either way I think the dog would look a lot less gormless if they actually got her groomed properly!!

September 19th

Dramas! Izzy and Em have fallen out with Megan. So they won't sit with her at lunch and they are totally airing her on Snapchat. Megan tried to go and sit with Maya and Maisie, but they totally didn't let her because she normally ignores them completely. She ended up sitting on her own - I've never really liked her so TBH I didn't really care when Em said none of us should sit with her.

Izzy is going out with Dan. I can't believe it. He's a bit of an idiot. Mind you I think she's only doing it to make Rob notice her. Dan might be an idiot, but he IS really good looking.

September 20th

Izzy is not going out with Dan - he called her a drama queen just because she cried twice in maths. Boys just don't get emotions AT ALL. I told her she should have listened to me when I told her he's an idiot. She spent the whole of break deleting pictures of him out of her phone.

Also, I don't know what went on yesterday but Megan and Maisie are now BFFs - their Instagram is all full of ILYSM comments for one another and Maya has been kicked out the group totally. They call themselves "The Ms," OMG so pathetic. I don't know who they think they are.

September 21st

The dog has got into the recycling bag and emptied the contents ALL over the garden!! I had to go out and sort her out, because she's got a plastic container (which previously had chicken breasts in it) stuck to her face and she kept turning round in circles trying to shake it off of her. She's always getting her head stuck in things. When she was really small she got her head wedged in the spokes of Neville's bike, and it was really hard to get her out. She also smashed into the glass doors at Auntie Sophie's about 4 times because she didn't realise they were glass and not an open door. Mind you Mum's done that before now after a few drinks and so has Auntie Sophie's husband Marc. Oh, and Neville.

Also when the puppy was new she used to follow Mum around EVERYWHERE and was always right near her feet. Mum was always treading on her head. Maybe that's why she isn't very bright?

PS: Izzy is back with Dan. Honestly!! If he dumps her again I won't have any sympathy.

PPS: She spent most of lunchtime taking loads of pictures with him to replace the ones she deleted.

PPPS: When I told Neville he said, "Why is she wasting her time with that cretin?" I didn't think he even knew who Dan is and I had to look up the word cretin. Neville also said, "She should have checked whether the pictures were still in her deleted folder on the phone. It usually stores them for about 30 days." I texted her to tell her that and they were still there! Then she was really annoyed because she missed out on roast dinner today while re-taking all the photos she had anyway. Like that's MY fault!

I made a comment about the dog not being very bright and Neville reckons it's been proved that dogs aren't even as intelligent as pigeons ... well that just says it all.

September 23rd

We went to Uncle Dave, Auntie Sally and my cousin Ella's for a BBQ and stayed over. We took the Idiot but their dog Flossie was not impressed - she hates our dog because our dog just chases her everywhere and won't leave her alone. Flossie gets really stressed out and tries to hide. She hides really badly - like in plain sight just facing a wall - so our dog just keeps on pestering her to play. In the end, I think she must have sneaked off upstairs, as the Idiot was just sitting on her own in the garden sulking.

Ella is 17 now, she is really, really cool and has a boyfriend called Danny (like a proper boyfriend - they actually go out with each other and everything). He has really good hair. She's told us she has decided that Ella is a rubbish name and she wants a cool name like some of her new college mates (that she calls fam). She said she tried to explain fam to Grandpa the other day, "I told him that it's like they're my family yeah? Close, like, my BFF's? Then Grandpa said, 'but we're your family'. So I told him, yeah but like that's biological - it's not like proper. So Grandpa shook his head and went into the kitchen muttering, 'biological is proper'.. and said they must be teaching us a load of rubbish in college."

Ella's new best mates in her fam are called Diamond, Riva and Chanice. So she's officially changed her name to Shanequa - you have to say it like Shan-E-quar. Grandma said it is bloody ridiculous and she is going to carry on calling her Ella. Shanequa said, "Yeah well, that's up to you Grandma but I might not answer." Neville mimicked her saying, "I might not answer" and added "innit an 'ting" on the end because he thought that was really funny. It's so NOT funny.

I hung out with Ella and Danny in her room which was fun since the adults all stayed outside until late drinking in the garden - we could hear them all laughing and being stupid. Then there was a big bang and loads more laughter. Turns out it was Mum, she'd walked straight into the patio door thinking it was open. That is just SO TYPICAL.

September 24th

We had a massive fry up at Uncle Dave's before coming home and then it was onto another party. Helen invited everyone round for one of their garden parties to make the most of the weather before it gets freezing!!!

We were all hanging out together at the end of the garden whilst the adults sat round on the patio drinking. It's only a matter of time before Helen suggests that they have tequila shots. It always gets messy quickly when that happens. The last time they had tequila Neville fell over in their front garden and bashed his head. Mind you he also had some disgusting drink from Poland they'd had in the cupboard for about 12 years - that probably didn't help!

When you listen to Neville tell stories about when he was young, it sounds like he has bashed his head loads of times.

He's no better than the dog.

Once when he was sledging, he apparently fell off his sledge and hit his back on the ground really hard and before he had time to get up a small child sledged over his head!! It's no wonder you can't get a sensible conversation out of him.

Mum can't drink tequila as it makes her feel sick - but whenever other people have it she always tells the same story about the time she saw this guy have a "Tequila Suicide" - even though everyone's heard it ! With normal tequilas you apparently drink the tequila, lick some salt off of your hand and squeeze some lemon in your mouth. I thought that was disgusting enough but the "suicide" version you drink the tequila, snort the salt up your nose and squeeze the lemon juice in your eye - it's completely insane. At least none of them are stupid enough to try that version. Not even Helen. Mum always tells the same stories like a MILLION times when she's drunk too much.

Mind you they all do that. The whole lot of them together are a nightmare - they all talk at once really loudly and you can't follow any of it. I think they should have a 'talking stick' like we used to have in infants school so everyone gets a chance. Jane was telling a mad story, which seemed to involve her getting on an international flight wearing only one shoe, that had them all screeching their heads off. Katie was trying to get everyone to dance on the lawn and Bridget got a phone call from home to say that her oldest son, even though he is 17, had somehow managed to get his head stuck in the banisters, so she had to leave early to sort him out.

Helen's husband cooked some really nice food on the BBQ and we all had really good fun. Luckily no one mentioned tequila, but they did start having Jaegerbombs which is almost as bad. Then they all started making complete idiots of themselves. When we left, Helen's husband had fallen asleep on the sofa, Katie was doing karaoke and dancing all on her own and Helen was rearranging the left over burgers and sausages into knobs. Totally embarrassing ….

I'm sooooo not drinking when I'm older.

September 25th

Mum is back on one of her health kicks. Probably because she spent yesterday eating all the rubbish in the house because she had a massive hangover. She claims it's all about "choosing nourishing food and listening to your body" and has nothing to do with eating crap for weeks on end!

I always know when she's on a health kick, because a load of weird stuff gets delivered from Ocado for Mum, and me and Neville have to make do with pasta and a bunch of cheap freezer meals from Tescos. There's loads of kale in the kitchen and weird packets of stuff like flaxseed and quinoa. Last time she got something called psyllium husk powder (!!???) to make special healthy gluten-free seeded bread. It just looked like a big bag of sand and only got used once - unsurprisingly it's not as nice as toast made with PROPER bread! She keeps saying she will make it again as it's full of antioxidants, but she just nicks all my bagels instead. Apparently the quinoa is pronounced keen-wah!! How stupid (and annoying) is that? Why can't you just say it like it looks?

I tried (for about the fourth time) to talk to Mum about all the stuff that I need - like a new brow kit - but she said we need to cut back on unnecessary spending and save a bit of money. I suggested she start by buying less Keen-wah!

Also there are no biscuits, or teacakes or any treaty things in the house!! Just because she keeps getting fatter doesn't mean we all have to suffer!! I've had a really stressful day actually and I'd like some biscuits. Izzy and Em made up with Megan and told her she's allowed to sit with them again if she wants to. I try not to get involved with all the drama because it's soooo stupid, but sometimes it's hard when that is ALL they are talking about.

Mum was listening to an annoying podcast about emotional eating and how people "react to various negative emotions by making poor food choices".. what a load of rubbish!! I was just about to tell her I thought it was rubbish when Izzy messaged to say that Megan (after speaking to Maisie) said she is never sitting with them again because they are 'boring and irrelevant' (Maisie's words) .... more drama .. I can't cope so I took the Idiot to the shops to get some Oreos to cheer myself up.

September 27th

Mum and Neville have been arguing for about an hour about getting a shed and what size it should be and where it should go in the garden. The garden isn't exactly big so it's either one corner or the other - how it could take that long to talk about I have no idea. Just pick a corner and get on with it. Adults' conversations are so pointless.

Maisie and Megan - or I should say 'The Ms' are walking around school like they own the place. SAD.

September 28th

Uncle John turned up unexpectedly on business - good timing because he gave me a £50 note for my birthday! We were all at Grandma's for lunch and Auntie Sophie had come over with my little nephew Felix, so Uncle John could meet him. It's the first time he's met him IRL and not on the screen! Felix is soooooo cute but he's really naughty. Mum said Auntie Sophie is doing sleep training with Felix from this book she has about 'contented babies'. It worked like clockwork on Coco who did everything she was supposed to do, but Felix is not taking any notice and is not going for his naps on schedule. Mum keeps saying, 'Gina Ford is a Nazi' (which is a bit irrelevant since no-one was talking about history and I have no idea who Gina Ford is anyway) and Grandma just rolled her eyes said, "I managed to raise five of you without reading any books and you all turned out all right."

We FaceTimed my little cousin Coco and Auntie Sophie's husband so Uncle John could chat to them. Auntie Sophie said she wanted remind Uncle Marc to MAKE SURE he puts Coco's new Gro Clock on so she knows when she is allowed to get up in the morning. Uncle John said, "Won't she just get up when she wants?" but Auntie Sophie said, "No that's the point of the Gro Clock, she can only get up when the clock tells her it's daytime." Uncle John said, "I thought she was a child genius? Surely she will see it's light outside?" Coco is a really bright little thing and Uncle John is always making jokes about it.

When we did the FaceTime Coco was supposed to be ready to go to bed but she was dancing around in the bedroom without any clothes on waving a glow stick. Auntie Sophie looked quite annoyed but was trying not to be in front of Uncle John. She said, "Marc, what's she doing with that glow stick? And has she had dinner and a bath yet?" and Uncle Marc said that he'd got her a kebab from the Turkish place on the way home earlier and that she wanted to have some sweets and a naked disco. He also said he hadn't had a chance to bath her yet. Auntie Sophie said bath time should have been at 6 o'clock and right now it is meant to be "quiet time" with a book. Then she said, "We will talk about this later" in a really firm voice.

She went off to change Felix's nappy and Uncle John said, "So... she's all hyped up on sugar, dancing round with no clothes on, she's had a kebab instead of some kind of kale and broccoli stew and hasn't been in the bath yet ... 10 quid says the Gro Clock isn't getting switched on tonight."

September 29th

It's my birthday in about 2 weeks time - I'm like one of the oldest in the year and I'm going to be a teenager!!!! Mind you, I wish Mum and Neville would stop making jokes about it and going on about "Kevin the Teenager" who was on TV years and years ago. It was really getting on my nerves but they found a clip on YouTube to show me and it was actually really funny. He was always shouting at his parents and stomping around the house saying "It's soooo UNFAIR, I HATE you" and swinging his arms around huffing and puffing. Neville does an impression of him every time I say I don't want to do something. That was funny for like a whole 30 seconds.

I'm so excited about my birthday - me and Em are having a joint party. I have got a really cool new dress.

Auntie Sophie posted in the family WhatsApp that Coco is having a little poem that she wrote at nursery published in a book. She said she didn't write the whole thing given that she's not quite 3 yet, but she had to give her ideas for it. Her ideas were mostly about Paw Patrol but it's a really cute poem. Everyone put congratulations or comments about how brilliant it is apart from Uncle John who said, "I'd have thought she'd be up for the Booker Prize by now?"

PS: Mum and Neville are still on about the shed. OMG. SO ANNOYING.

September 30th

Em stayed for a sleepover last night and we've spent all afternoon practicing our dance routine for the school talent show. I think it's brilliant and Mum agreed. She was working on her computer all afternoon again, so Neville and his mate took the dogs for a walk but that was hours ago and he's still not back. He's usually only gone for about 20 minutes so it must mean they've walked to the pub and stayed there. He likes to go on Sundays because they leave all the left over roast potatoes from the restaurant on the bar and people can just help themselves.

Em went home earlier and I've just woken up from a big nap - we didn't get to bed until 3am last night so I am soooooooooo tired. When I got downstairs Mum was complaining about Neville. He'd been down the pub all afternoon with Helen's husband and obviously had loads of beer. He was staggering around the kitchen pretending he wasn't drunk. He decided to try and mow the lawn to prove his point but he was stumbling about the garden and nearly garrotted himself on the washing line. Mum said one of these days he'll probably mow straight over the lawnmower cable and electrocute himself ….. then she texted Helen to see if was just Neville or if her husband was in the same sort of state. Turned out he was. He'd gone into the garden to pretend to do something useful as well, but had managed to trip over a paving stone and fall face first into the shed.

That's EXACTLY what will happen to Neville if we get a shed.

I spent the rest of the evening in my room.

October 3rd

Mum is having another rant about President Trump - she hates him and says he's a dangerous fascist and keeps muttering about slippery slopes and history repeating itself whatever that means. I don't really like history so I don't pay much attention to it in school - mainly because Miss Davies has a really slow boring voice that kind of makes you lose concentration. Neville just says he's amazed no-one has shot Trump yet and that "someone should prise his phone from his tiny little hands and delete his Twitter account." All I know is that he has really ridiculous hair and his wife always looks very unhappy. Mum keeps saying that between him and our excuse for a Prime Minister that it's a shame Spitting Image is no longer around as they would have a field day. Spitting Image was apparently some programme with puppets that were made to look like politicians - must have been horrible to watch as all the politicians are really ugly apart from this one nice one in Canada. Anyway it was really funny according to Mum and Neville.

"Have a field day" - that's another expression Mum uses a lot and Grandma uses even more. What's a field day? Is it a day in a field? Who would want to spend a day in a field? Probably Mum, if she could walk around barefoot chanting stuff. Neville says the only times he's ever spent a day in a field were at Glastonbury and most of that involved queuing for the portaloos. He said when you get in the actual portaloo it's like there's been an explosion in a shit factory and it's almost impossible to breath, especially in summer. Ugghghgh, I don't think I will ever go to a festival unless I can do the glamping version. Neville is always reminiscing about Glastonbury. He went lots when he was younger, he used to have really long straggly hair, I've seen tons of his old photos and they are really funny (mainly because he's so bald now).

Also he thinks he's a rock star!!! SAD!! He is in this band called
Chemical Banana - he thinks it's a great name because he thought it
up, but it's just really really cringe. And they are absolutely terrible.
It's so embarrassing as they play in the pubs in our town and all my
friends know about them. They are all really old and I don't even
know any of the songs. Neville's about the youngest one in the band.
One of them (Pete) is totally bald on the top of his head but has
grown the rest of his hair long and has this really sad straggly grey
ponytail!!! Mum says there are only ever about 5 people that go and
watch them and that two of them are the bar staff who don't have
any choice. There's also this really sad old woman that is obsessed
with Pete and always turns up drunk and dances right in front of him.
Mum says she's the sort of person that Grandma calls "mutton
dressed as lamb". Neville always comes back really happy from his
gigs saying that the pub was packed and the place was "rocking".
Seriously unlikely!

I need to remember to ask Grandma what mutton dressed as lamb
actually is ….

October 4th

Mum has noticed me writing in my journal a fair bit and keeps
smiling to herself about it... like it was all her idea and I wouldn't
have thought of it by myself. Honestly. She started on about
gratitude journals again - some stupid thing she is ALWAYS going
on about where you write down all the things you are grateful for,
then apparently, you will instantly be happier because you realise
how much good stuff you have in your life. An "attitude of
gratitude" she calls it. That's annoying. Just because it rhymes
doesn't make it a better saying. I tried to tell her my journal is more
the things I'm NOT grateful for - mainly because they annoy me!

She wasn't really listening as usual - she was rattling on about how focusing on gratitude keeps you grounded in the "NOW". She has a thing about that - she read some book that said there is no past and no future and there is only the present moment - that's all we have. Well that's a load of rubbish for a start!! There's yesterday and tomorrow. I know this because yesterday I had to go for a cross country run at school (which was hideous) and tomorrow I'm going to Costa with Izzy (which will be brilliant). So ... if there literally was ONLY the present moment - which is basically Mum annoying me - then life would be a nightmare.

October 5th

I came home from Costa and had another moan about the fact that EVERYONE has a better phone that I do - I only want an iPhone 7 - it's not much to ask - loads of people have got iphoneX's. Mum and Neville just don't get it. I tried to explain about how much it matters but it didn't do any good (as usual). Even Megan has one and her family have hardly any money. Neville laughed when I said that and said, "Well they have enough money for a 75in HD TV - her dad was boasting about it down the pub last week."

First Neville went on and on about how in his day we didn't even have phones or TVs... he always goes off on a rant about how tough it was but they had fun and spent time outside and used their imaginations.. God it's soooooooooo boring. I think I could actually repeat this speech he says it so often.

THEN I got a lecture from Mum about how we should all walk our own path and not feel that we have to compete with anyone else. Mum said we shouldn't be comparing our lives to those of other people on Instagram, because that is not reality and we are only seeing their "highlights reel" and not the everyday stuff they go through. Then she went into a rant about Chloe's mum, Jasmine. Jasmine drives a massive 4x4 and is stunningly pretty and wears the coolest clothes. Her and her friends are always hanging out in the coffee shop and they all have fabulous semi-permanent eye lashes, HD brows and amazing nails. Mum is just jealous because her stomach hangs over her trousers and her hair is going grey. Stalking Jasmine's Facebook profile doesn't help - so many perfect photos of her looking super skinny - it just puts Mum in a bad mood but she still does it, ALL THE TIME!! Some days, she'll start making a mood board on what she is going to do to get the perfect body. That's a joke, as she's always going on about the fact that the media is "indoctrinating us with diet culture" and everyone should love themselves just as they are.

She also stalks someone called Louise that she doesn't even like. They were at school together a million years ago and haven't even met again IRL … It's been particularly bad the last week because Louise has just been on THE most amazing holiday to the Maldives. Mum has spent a ton of time looking at all her photos - which are utterly amazing actually - and being really snappy with me as a result. Then after a few days of sulking she announced that getting the things you desire in life is simple because when you are "in the right headspace and living at a high enough vibration you can just manifest them". Then she muttered something about being a manifesting machine and stuck a picture of a 5 star Maldives resort on the fridge.

I told Grandma how Mum is always going on about Jasmine and Grandma said, "Oooooh, a touch of the green eyed monster if you ask me" and then wanted to know if Jasmine is one of those 'yummy mummies' - that is such an annoying expression and even more annoying because she actually made air quotes with her hands when she said it. Urgghghh - Cringe!

Debbie's oldest child has broken his ankle and the youngest one has chicken pox. She also put a close up photo of her husband's fungal toenail infection on Facebook. Neville just said, "What is wrong with that woman?" and walked out of the room.

October 6th

Neville has got a new boss - he isn't happy and has been going on about it night after night for the last week. He's 25, his name's Ollie and he has a beard and a man-bun. Neville came home ranting about him and muttering things about hipsters and entitled millennials. He says that hipsters look ridiculous with their skinny trousers and excessive facial hair. Ollie is new to this section of the company, and he's come through a university graduate training programme. Neville said that doesn't mean he should be given such a senior position.

Neville is just jealous because he wanted the job, he's always ranting on about the fact that qualifications are a waste of time and he went to the University of Life - that annoys me. That's not a thing.

I think Ollie sounds really nice - apparently he spent his gap year looking after orphans with diseases in India which I think is really kind. I told Neville he was being unfair and that I thought it was lovely of Ollie to give up his holiday time to look after people that were suffering. Neville just looked annoyed and said, "Yes he's a f**king saint, I expect he found a cure for leprosy while he was at it." Mum told Neville that he ought to show a bit more caring towards his fellow man, and that if he had actually experienced the horror of poverty in the 3rd world first hand, he wouldn't say such awful things.

I didn't know what leprosy is - I had to google it. It sounds disgusting!!! Ollie must be mad - if I have a gap year I'm going to spend it getting a tan and meeting lots of Australian surfers.

October 7th

OMG - it's my birthday party in just over 1 week and Neville just suggested that instead of having a disco and playing the absolutely BRILLIANT Spotify playlist that me, Em and Izzy have spent FOREVER putting together, that it would be better to have live music.

He ACTUALLY suggested that Chemical Banana play a "one-off birthday gig". He thinks that will make all my friends think that I am incredibly cool and get me what he called some "serious clout with the popular kids."

I am not often lost for words, but didn't know what to say - good job Mum came in at just the right moment and laughed her head off. She said, "For goodness sake Neville, do you want the poor child to be a laughing stock?"

For once I felt like Mum actually gets me - then she ruined it by saying, "Yeah, having Neville perform to impress your friends - it's not exactly #squadgoals is it?"

OMG I can't believe she said that. Even worse she actually SAID the word "hashtag" as well!!!!!

October 8th

Here we go again... decluttering has reached a new (totally extreme) level! Mum is now into something called "Minimalism" - she saw a documentary on Netflix about how "getting rid of all your material possessions and living with less is the key to a simplified and happy life." Not sure where the "happy" bit comes in since it's turned her into a monster!! She is rampaging around the house getting rid of loads of stuff! I've shut my bedroom door and barricaded it with a chair so she can't take any of my stuff out. She has a massive pile of my DVDs for the charity shop - I was upset at first but actually there isn't much point in keeping them because I can just watch them on Netflix anyway.

Things that have gone so far today ....

A bookshelf that never had anything on it ..

After Mum bought this bookshelf (that she didn't need in the first place) she was going to buy a load of stuff she didn't need to put on it. Then she decided material possessions are not the answer and we are apparently all living in The Matrix (whatever that is) where we are materialistic zombies hopelessly staring at our phones all day and getting brainwashed by endless advertising which makes us mindlessly purchase and consume things without questioning our choices…. Whatever!

Other things that have gone today …

- • Another book shelf that did have books on it but they are now at the charity shop so it's empty
- • More books from a box in the office
- • The Penny Board I used once
- • The Heeley shoes I wore once
- • The wellington boots I wore once
- • The clumpy trainers I wore once (Mum bought them cheap and I hated them - I asked for Adidas not Tescos!!!!!! She is so out of touch)
- • Neville's water filter jug he never uses
- • Neville's pancake maker
- • Neville's bread maker
- • Neville's waffle maker
- • Neville's latte maker
- • Neville's caffetiere
- • MY popcorn maker (no one asked me!!) but actually I never use it, I just get the microwave stuff …..
- • A load of baskets with nothing in that Mum always said would come in handy one day (they haven't)
- • 4 pointless lamps we never use
- • 5 pointless ornaments
- • 2 hideous jugs that were a gift from someone
- • Broken chiminea Neville was going to fix
- • Broken chair Neville was going to fix
- • Broken coffee table Neville was going to fix
- • Broken blind Neville was going to fix
- • Broken outdoor bench Neville was going to fix

- • 24 ramekin dishes from the kitchen - who needs that many little round things?????
- • Loads of mugs with stupid things written on them
- • The old kettle that doesn't work anyway
- • The old iron that doesn't work anyway
- • The old dog gate that doesn't work anyway
- • The old drill that doesn't work anyway
- • The old toaster that doesn't work anyway
- • Practically ALL of Mum's clothes
- • Anything of Neville's that Mum never liked him wearing (which is A LOT !!!)

All this has apparently reduced her stress levels and made her feel lighter and really, really content.

October 10th

Mum is ranting about having no clothes to wear.

October 11th

I let Mum calm down a bit over night and then earlier on I suggested that we go to Primark so she can pick up a few bits so she has some stuff to wear. It was a bit sneaky, as I knew once we got in there I'd be able to persuade her to get me some stuff too. I totally need some new make-up for the party.

Ha - that worked brilliantly - Mum seemed very happy being a consumer of material goods and I came home with two massive paper bags of new stuff.

October 13th

It's my birthday - I'm finally a teenager!! Shame I have to go to school but it's my fabulous party later!!! YAAAAASSSSSS!

Megan and Maisie were talking about me and Em in the canteen at lunch. I could totally tell because they were shooting me the death stare. I told Em "Megan is giving me the look." She said, "Is it the look? or THE look?" I said definitely "THE look", it's because they didn't get an invite to the party. I don't care - I don't want them there.

Neville was ranting about Ollie again when I got home. I had a cup of tea with Mum and he started.

"So Jaz - it turns out Ollie's a vegan. How do I know that?? Hmmm? Hmmm? Cos he bloody well told me didn't he? And everyone else in the meeting and the girls on reception and the f**king DPD delivery bloke. Why do these people feel the need to run round telling everyone they are a vegan? I don't go round telling every Tom, Dick and Harry I meet that I'm a f**king carnivore do I."

Mum was saying, "Don't worry about it Neville. YOU don't have to become a vegan - it's not compulsory you know. I've got no idea why it annoys you so much. If people want to do something that causes less suffering to animals, what's the harm in that? To be honest, with the state of the planet and the increased consciousness of the individual, I expect veganism is the future..."

Neville said, "Well the future can piss right off."

I was glad to have an excuse to get out of the kitchen - I needed to get started on party preparations - my make-up needs to be seriously amazing for tonight.

October 14th

I spent most of the day asleep - I was soooooooo tired after last night's sleep over. We all stayed up really, really late talking about the party.

OMG - the party was amazing!!!! Everyone looked soooooooooo gorgeous!! My dress was perfect.

Loads happened too. Em and James A. are now going out. Also Izzy and Connor ... Dan is NOT impressed. Charlotte and Daniel and Alice and Ben.

I was too busy taking photos and posting everything onto Snapchat and Instagram to find a boyfriend. So many amazing photos - everyone commented on them.

Also Sarah W, Asha and Kaleigh are all Lesbians now apparently. I don't think it's because of the party though. It's just when they decided to tell people. Mum said she already knew because Jane had put something about it on WhatsApp, although initially it autocorrected from Lesbians to Africans so they were all a bit confused.

Oscar and India aren't a thing anymore - which is actually quite funny because India said they were completely in LOVE yesterday and none of us believed her. Oscar said she's too posh for him anyway - that's a joke since he is the poshest boy in school!!! According to Neville his dad owns some multi-million dollar tech company and says the only reason he goes to our crappy school and not Eton is because his Mum is a Labour MP and she doesn't want to look like she isn't supporting her own party's views.

I don't know much about politics and TBH I'm not really interested. People seem to get too worked up when they talk about it and end up falling out with each other. Mum, Auntie Eleanor and Uncle John are a really good example. They are all officially not allowed to talk about Donald Trump after Uncle John's last visit … what a nightmare THAT was!!!

I also don't know Oscar's dad's real name either since Neville only ever calls him "that pretentious bellend"

October 15th

We all went to Grandma's so I could have a birthday lunch and (more importantly) another cake! It was also to get more presents from the family - I got tons of really great stuff. Shanequa got me a body con dress from Missguided; Grandma got me some winter boots; Auntie Sophie got me a really really cool Urban Decay eyeshadow pallet and I got the best Birthday hug from Coco who just hung on to me for ages.

Auntie Eleanor sent me a card which said my birthday money had been donated to a charity for refugees. So the next child refugee arriving in a boat, to wherever they can get to, would get a warm coat, a sleeping bag and a full survival pack.

The house smelt lovely when we got there because Grandma had baked a homemade cake for me, but then Felix did a massive poo which came out the side of his nappy and went all down his leg and up his back and the smell of that kind of took over. He thought it was really funny and just kept laughing while Auntie Sophie wrestled him into a clean outfit. It looked like a pretty revolting job if you ask me!

Coco was eating a really healthy little snack of homemade hummus, carrot sticks and mini rice cakes. Mum turned to me and said, "When you were that age I used to give you little tupperware containers of Cheerios and Coco Pops." And she has the cheek to rattle on about healthy food - it's a miracle my immune system works.

Grandpa was making tea for everyone when Uncle Dave, Auntie Sally and Shanequa arrived. Shanequa brought Danny along too. Grandpa said, "Hello young man" to him and he said, "Ayt Bruh. Everyfing good yeah?" Grandpa just looked a bit confused and went off to see if the tea had infused for 6 minutes. He's very fussy about his tea. When he brought the pot back in Danny said, "Nah allow it, I rate tea." Grandpa just looked even more confused and started to do the crossword.

Coco did a really cute little dance for us and we all cheered at the end and Auntie Sophie took a video to put on WhatsApp.

Grandma was asking Shanequa if she's enjoying college and she said, "You know what though Grandma, I thought I was done but I'm like SO done, too much adulting yeah?" It was Grandma's turn to look confused and she went off to get the cake sorted out for us to have a slice with our tea.

Grandpa decided to have a chat with Danny;

G: So young man, how long have you been dating my lovely granddaughter now then?

D: Like it's 4 months now innit? She's the best Bruh, like she's my pengting - yeah?

G: What's a pengting?

D: What do you mean?

G: I mean what is it? What does the word actually mean?

D: It's like something really attractive, like pretty... like looks really good yeah?

Grandma came in right then with my cake which looked sooooo lovely. So Grandpa pointed at it and said, "So is that a pengting then?" and Danny said, "Nah Bruh, that's a CAKE."

Grandpa just shook his head and ignored Danny for the rest of the day.

We had dinner later on and it was really nice, although Felix threw most of his on the floor. Auntie Sophie they are doing "baby-led weaning" which is where the baby chooses what food to pick up and eat and you don't try to feed them. Grandpa said, "Babies aren't supposed to lead anything. They are supposed to be shown what to do. That's just a bloody waste of good food if you ask me. What a load of modern crap! "

Then Coco shouted 'crap' really loudly. Auntie Sophie told her off. It didn't work very well because everyone else was laughing, so she just ran round shouting "crap, crap, crap" over and over.

October 16th

My party is now old news. Dan picked a fight with Connor at lunch because of Izzy. It was all very dramatic but it didn't last long as they both got separated by some older boys and then Mr Warner put them both in detention. Izzy decided she thought it was romantic of Dan ... romantic?? Seriously?? She is totally watching the wrong films! Anyway she is now going back out with Dan. Me and Em totally can't keep up with it.

I put load more party photos on Insta and Snapchat to get people talking about the party again.

OMG. Mum and Neville have started on about the shed again. There's now some talk about whether it should be a summerhouse. I really don't care.

October 17th

I'm spending more time in my room writing in this journal in the evenings as Mum and Neville seem to be spending hours shouting at one another. Neville is just in SUCH a bad mood these days and Mum thinks it's because of how much he detests working for Ollie!

I'm worried they might get divorced. Loads of people's parents are divorced in my class alone, never mind my year!! Jack, Connor, Fern, Elizabeth, Kyle, Amelie, Freya, both James 1 & 2 and Charlotte.

I really really hope her and Neville don't get divorced - he annoys me a lot but I wouldn't like it if he wasn't around.

Grandma always says that these days young people don't seem to understand the meaning of things like compromise and commitment. She said in her day people stayed together even if they were really miserable because life's not all 'fun and games'. It's really confusing - Mum is always saying the opposite - that we all deserve to be happy because life is short and people shouldn't stay in situations that make them miserable.

I decided to ring Grandma as I was feeling a bit upset and confused and she said not to worry. She said them shouting at each other was perfectly normal and doesn't mean they are going to split up. She said it's healthy to have a good row and get it out of your system. She also said I'd want to worry if they didn't ever have an argument because people like that 'aren't normal.'

I was feeling better until she added, "Then again they might split up … people these days get divorced at the drop of a hat."

It was an odd thing to say because neither Neville nor Mum have got a hat... well except for a comedy one that looks like a turkey that Neville always wears for Christmas dinner. Neville doesn't need a hat anyway - he's got about 4,000 Chemical Banana bandanas that he had printed on Ebay that no one wants to buy. They are in a big box in the cupboard under the stairs and Magda our cleaner keeps using them to dust round the house which really annoys Neville

The other day Neville was absolutely furious because he found one of them lying in the garden with what he described as "a massive steaming dog turd" on top of it !!

Mum said she thought that was actually an "incredible piece of symbolic artwork" and that "maybe the dog is way more intellectual than any of us realises."

October 19th

I bought a swegway with ALL my savings.

Oh and Dan dumped Izzy. In the canteen. In front of LOADS of people. He said it's because she's always crying. She said that was total rubbish and then burst into tears and spent the whole day crying. It was a TOTAL drama! I was in the middle of telling Mum ALL about it when Neville walked in. He just said, "I know, don't tell me, Izzy threw another wobbly"... I giggled about that for ages. "Throwing a wobbly" is a really weird expression but I actually really like it.

Good job it's half term next week - she can avoid Dan for a week.

October 21st

So... today Neville broke my swegway. I hardly had time to try it out!!!!

He'd been in the pub all afternoon with Mark, Dave and Andy. When he got back he insisted that he was making dinner as he CLAIMED he wasn't drunk. Mum went upstairs to have a long bath and some "me time" and left him to it. I had my dinner early and went to bed. According to Mum, when she came downstairs he was smashing around the kitchen, on MY swegway, with his headphones on wearing this ridiculous big coloured scarf and banging into the cupboards and the bin and the table and everything. The scarf is apparently the same as the one worn by Doctor Who millions of years ago, before they decided the next Doctor Who is going to be a woman. Mum's friend Helga knitted the scarf because her and Neville are both fans of The Doctor and talk about all sorts of rubbish to do with Science Fiction (or "Sci-Fi shit" as Mum calls it). Mum says he looks like a right burke in the scarf. He looks like a right burke in most things as far as I can tell.

I.AM.SO.ANGRY.I.COULD.SCREAM

October 22nd

I am no longer angry with Neville. I shouted at him A LOT this morning, so he googled a fix for the swegway - when they get bashed they can get out of alignment and need to be sort of rebooted! He managed to do this. Thank goodness. So anyway it's working again but he is not allowed to get on it EVER AGAIN.

I went off for a long bath this evening because I needed to put a deep conditioning mask on my hair and let it soak in for a bit - that way my hair will look amazing for tomorrow. Me and Em are going shopping. We might ask Izzy - depends if she wants to talk about Dan and Connor. I'm so done with that.

There was some weird gadget thing left on the sink in the bathroom. Apparently it is something that Neville uses to trim his nose and ear hair!!!! That's sooooo revolting! He kept making jokes about turning into a hobbit - though that doesn't make much sense as hobbits are really small and Neville is quite tall.

I read The Hobbit at school. It's supposed to be a classic novel but I thought it was boring. It's just about this little creature with hairy feet that finds a magic ring or something. Total rubbish. Neville always rants about it and goes on about Peter Jackson having no business dragging it out into three films (whoever Peter Jackson is). There is a follow up story called The Lord of the Rings and that is Neville's favourite film - well three films. For some reason it's OK for that one to be three films. I don't know why.

Whenever Neville mentions the Lord of the Rings it makes Mum go off on one of her travel reminiscing rambles. Apparently it was all filmed in New Zealand. Her and Auntie Sophie went there together when she was younger and did lots of cool stuff like skydiving and swimming with dolphins. She always looks a bit sad when she tells her stories about travelling round the world. I think she misses it. She has loads of places she still wants to go to. Her latest obsession is dream boards. There are pictures of exotic places stuck all round the house and all over the office. She saw something about it on the internet and did an all day workshop on it. Seems a bit of a pointless workshop to me - I could have told her to go to google images and print out a bunch of pictures she liked. Whoever ran the workshop must be "laughing all the way to the bank" as Grandma always says.

But Mum says that I don't get it and there's a lot more to it than just pinning a bunch of photos to a board. She says you have to "visualise all the stuff you want to do in life and live at a high vibration" and it will all magically happen. If living at a high vibration is the same as shouting at me she should be really good at it!!!

She's been trying to print out a picture of the Northern Lights for the last half an hour but the printer keeps jamming. There is A LOT of swearing coming from the office and a load of ranting about something called Mercury Retrograde. I don't know what she is talking about but we learnt about mercury and thermometers in science so it must be something to do with temperature. She keeps on about hot flushes all the time so maybe it's that. Apparently that is something to do with the menopause which happens to women when they get older. Neville says it's all about hormones and that women get "even more irrational and mental than normal ...... if that's even possible." Mum told him off for saying that and said there is a huge amount of stigma around mental illness and it's not something to make jokes about.

Neville sorted out the printer - he's really good at that stuff. Mum refers to him as her "IT department" because she's self-employed. That annoys me!!!

Apparently we are going to Iceland in about a year and we might actually see the Northern Lights. I'm not sure printing a picture out after you've booked a holiday to the place in the photo really counts as successful visualising, but what do I know???

Neville keeps saying, "Iceland the country, not Iceland the place you can buy a prawn ring". It was vaguely amusing the first time, but now it really annoys me.

Things that annoy me about Neville

* When he breaks my stuff

* When he makes jokes and I don't find them funny... but he thinks they are hilarious

* When he keeps making the same joke when it's totally obvious it's NOT funny

* When he laughs at his own jokes (still not funny)

* The fact that he listens to Radio 2 - this is really annoying in the car

* The fact that he listens to Radio 2 - also annoying outside the car

* When he gets really angry in the car and swears at other drivers

* When he gets annoyed that I won't wear the Chemical Banana T-shirt he had specially printed for me - like I EVER would

* The fact he is even IN Chemical Banana

October 23rd

It's half term - I'm going to Grandma's for few days.

October 25th

I forgot my journal while I was at Grandma's. I quite missed writing in it.

Anyway it was nice at Grandma's - she always spoils me and takes me shopping. We went to New Look and she got me a really snuggly dressing gown and slippers. We watched the Bake Off final on catch-up (even though I already knew who the winner was) and re-runs of Friday Night Dinner (which Grandma and Grandpa LOVE) and Grandpa made me hot chocolate before bed every night. Grandma made me some really nice dinners. We had steak and jacket potatoes one night - I love that and we NEVER have it at home. Mum pretends it's because she doesn't want to support the killing of cattle and because she's experimenting with veganism (she isn't). It's really because beef is expensive. She will happily support the killing of cattle when Grandma makes roast beef and yorkshires!

October 26th

I wish we'd gone on holiday. Everyone else is having "winter sun" holidays. Izzy is in Gran Canaria, Em has gone to Egypt, Oscar is in the Caribbean. Mum and Neville have both been working so I've been totally BORED! And I'm avoiding Instagram because I'm SO SICK of everyone's sunny holiday photos! At least being at Grandma's for a few days got me away from Mum going on and on about Chloe's family being in Dubai. She said, "If I see one more picture of Jasmine drinking cocktails and showing off her designer shoes and handbags I will scream." If she didn't stalk Jasmine's profile all day she wouldn't have to see ANY photos at all - she seems to have misunderstood that simple fact!!

I also pointed out that buying designer clothes and handbags were surely examples of being a mindless consumer and not in keeping with her views about minimalism. She told me to shut up as she was on hold with O2 about a phone upgrade.

October 27th

Neville has been complaining to Mum for about an hour about Ollie and the fact his father is financing a trendy vegan cafe as "a little business sideline" for him. Apparently Ollie used to go to somewhere similar when his family lived in Shoreditch and feels there's a gap in the market. Ollie apparently said our town doesn't offer anywhere for "modern health conscious youngsters to find good, locally sourced, organic food." He said he wants to "create somewhere where eating is a sensual experience, with a minimalist, inclusive environment that promotes global values of sustainability and food independence."

Neville said, "I don't know what he's banging on about half the time, it's like listening to another f**king language." Mum said she thought it would be great to have somewhere to get a healthy salad for lunch instead of going to Tescos or Subway, but Neville said, "It'll be all edible kale napkins, deconstructed baked beans and bowls of stuff that looks like it should be in a bird feeder." Mum started to comment about the nutritional value of superfoods, but he carried on ranting, "Well, I won't be seen dead in there, Jaz. And I won't be lining Ollie's pockets thank you very much. You won't catch me eating a load of pretentious crap served on a shovel by a smug, beardy hipster."

I asked him who serves things on shovels, as it's just a ridiculous thing to say but he just replied, "You mark my words Ruby, you'll see."

October 30th

Debbie's other child has chicken pox now and the one with the broken ankle threw up all over his cast. She put a picture of it on Facebook before she even cleaned it up. OMG!

I asked Mum what the Appleby's were up to (just to wind her up) and seriously wish that I hadn't! Mrs Appleby has made the most incredible Halloween outfits for the twins, the whole outside of the house and garden has been decorated with these amazing ghosts and lanterns. She has put some kind of thin white stuff that looks like cobwebs all over the trees and bushes. They've had a family competition to see who could carve the most intricate pumpkin and she's been baking Halloween treats all week. There are spider cupcakes and eyeballs and these amazing things that look like severed fingers made out of marzipan. We've done nothing for Halloween. AS USUAL.

Neville just said, "What a load of bollocks - we shouldn't even have to celebrate Halloween - more American shite."

Mum did actually carve me a pumpkin one year - she got it in plenty of time and carved a really cool face in it (copied off of Pinterest) then we went away for a few days. When we got back ready to put it in the window for Halloween, she'd forgotten to turn off the central heating and left it near a radiator, so it had gone all mouldy and it's face had collapsed. I was really upset as I was quite young, but Mum thought it was really funny and put a picture on Facebook. Even her friend Margaret wrote under the photo, "You really are a terrible mother."

November 1st

So as usual Halloween was a bit rubbish. Mum and Neville turned all the lights out on the 31st so no one would knock on the door. I went trick or treating for a bit with Alice and Em, but it wasn't as much fun as usual because it was a school night and we couldn't do a sleep over afterwards. Mum doesn't agree with trick or treating - she says it's us being indoctrinated with more traditions that have no basis in our own cultural history.

Mum said she is sick of arguing with Neville about the shed. He wants it to be some kind of "man cave" where he can drink beer and get away from us (well Mum mainly). He said it will save him a f**king fortune, as at the moment he has to go to the pub every time he needs a bit of peace.

Mum said she has seen these amazing "She Sheds" on the internet that are all cosy with cushions, snuggly blankets and fairy lights. She said, "There are some great ideas online and it would be the perfect place for me to create a sacred space, where I can recharge my energy and establish a proper meditation practice."

But Neville said, "Yeah well, my beer drinking practice is already fully established, so it makes far more sense for it be a man cave."

I couldn't care less what it is, I just want them to stop going on about it. They could win some kind of record for talking about something SO BORING for such a long time!

November 5th

Went to the town firework night with Izzy, Em, Megan and Alice - it was really good. Loads of people were moaning about the stress it was causing their pets. When I got home I asked Mum if the dog had got upset and she said she'd spent the whole night laid out on her back, on the sofa, not even remotely bothered!! I don't think she is bright enough to be scared of things. She apparently barked at the window a couple of times but I think that's because it's dark now since the clocks went back and she doesn't realise that the dog she can see in the reflection is actually her and not another dog !

Mum was swearing at her phone when I got back. I asked her what was up and she said, "Debbie's attention seeking again - she's put on some vague post saying "OMG, worst day ever, why are people like that???" She only does it just so people will ask her what is wrong. One of the kids is bound to be ill! "

I pointed out that if the kids were actually ill she'd definitely have mentioned it and probably included a photo of whatever the illness involved.

Mum said, "That's true, but anyway I'm not going to rise to it and ask her what the matter is. I absolutely hate 'vague-booking.'

I told her I absolutely hate people using the word 'vague-booking.' SO ANNOYING.

Turns out Debbie was upset because the fireworks had scared her dog, so she'd complained about it and a whole load of people had had a right go at her because it's bonfire night tomorrow and she shouldn't be moaning about people having fun even if it did upset the dog. Neville said, "Well I've got no sympathy for the stupid woman, if she didn't know there would be a load of noise when the town firework display is taking place in the field right next to her house, then she's even more stupid than she appears most days on Facebook."

Also the Applebys have changed their cover photo to one of them all in matching "Appleby Adventures" branded beany hats with Mr Appleby writing the word "Love" in the sky with a sparkler … I thought it was clever, but it put Neville in a very bad mood.

November 6th

Arrghghgh so tired this morning going back to school. Got up late and didn't have time to put my make-up on - total nightmare!!! Mum was arguing with Neville in the kitchen saying that if he wasn't prepared to let her have the shed for her "sacred meditation area" she'd re-arrange the room where he plays on his Xbox and set up an area in there.

He said, "If you de-clutter a damn thing from that room whilst I am at work you'll find all your crystals down the f**king toilet."

Honestly I'm sure other parents don't have conversations like that! Although Amelie said when her parents were getting divorced her Mum cut one sleeve off of every single one of her Dad's work jackets and work shirts. I said that was terrible, but she said it was revenge because he'd sold a pair of her designer shoes on Ebay!!

November 9th

So tired (again!) this morning. I slept really badly because there was a whole bunch of noise going on downstairs really late last night - this usually means that Mum is doing something or other!! Turns out I was right - when I went down this morning she had rearranged ALL the furniture in the lounge instead (or what's left of the furniture since her Minimalism phase). It's all to do with something called Feng Shui apparently.

When I got in from school she explained that according to Feng Shui, things have to be in certain places for the correct energy to flow through the house. She says there are different areas of the house that represent prosperity and creativity and travel and all sorts of other stuff and everything has to be arranged in a certain way. Mum keeps tutting and moving my bag of stinky PE kit out of the 'prosperity corner.' She was trying to explain it all to me but I stopped listening to her and starting scrolling through my Instagram feed instead. Unsurprisingly she didn't notice.

Mum is putting strange objects in certain bits of the house like plants and Goddess statues and weird piles of rocks. There are things in 'lucky' colours apparently and we have keep everything tidy so the energy in the house stays fresh.

Neville said he had a curry for lunch and the unpleasant effect it's having on his stomach won't keep the energy in the house fresh for very long.

Turns out this wasn't a joke. He stinks more than the dog right now. I spent the rest of the night in my room.

November 11th

Uncle Dave, Auntie Sally and Shanequa came for the weekend and they brought Flossie over. Flossie was NOT impressed - I think she would actually have preferred to go into kennels - THAT is how much she hates our dog. She sought refuge under the kitchen table for a while, but the Idiot soon hounded her out of there.

Flossie was so pissed off she did a MASSIVE protest poo in the prosperity corner. I don't know much about Feng Shui, but I don't think that's a very good sign. Uncle Dave insisted that he'd clean it up but Mum started stress cleaning like she always does if she's annoyed, but I think she just wanted to get the poo out of her 'spiritual realm' asap. Poor Flossie was sent outside, with the Idiot. I wished her luck, took some crisps and me and Shanequa went up to my room to hang out.

Mum and Sally spent ages talking about all the Feng Shui stuff - Sally is a bit like Mum, she is interested in all that stuff - she likes

Reiki and Tarot cards and lots of other things that Grandpa calls 'bloody nonsense.'

Auntie Sophie Facetimed later for a chat since we were all together so Felix and Coco could wave at us. They like seeing the dog so we normally lift her up so they can see her. Even when Coco calls her name she can't work out it's coming from the screen so they usually just see a furry object looking gormlessly in another direction.

Auntie Sophie is not very happy with Uncle Marc - he was supposed to be home early last night, because they had a big family morning out planned today. He ended up sleeping in because he had a big hangover and then they were really late leaving the house. He called to say he was on his way home last night and should have been home in about 10 minutes. Apparently it took him about 2 hours to get home and when he finally arrived he'd had lots of rum and was wearing two coats, neither of which were his!

November 12th

Neville has gone to see his dad for the day. He often goes on a Sunday to see him. He is in an old people's home which is a bit sad. I've been a couple of times but he doesn't really know who I am so it's a bit weird. Neville's mum died around the time Mum and Neville met, I was only really little so I don't remember her at all. I only know her from the photos that Neville has, she looks really lovely. She had a big heart attack one day. His Dad was in their old home for a while but he started to forget things and then he set fire to something in the kitchen because he left the stove on, so he got moved to a home where he'd be a bit safer. Neville says he has something called Dementia which is a horrible disease where old

71

people don't recognise anyone and don't know what is going on. Sometimes they can get angry and violent but Neville's dad is happy most of the time. He doesn't really realise he is in a home, he thinks he is on a farm like the one he lived on when he was very young. I think that's kind of nice.

Neville looked a bit sad when he got back - I heard him telling Mum that his dad kept calling him Gerald. He has never heard of a Gerald so it probably means that his Dad is starting not to know who he is. We didn't really see him for the rest of the night - he went off to play on his Xbox with his headphones on so we didn't disturb him and when he finally came out his eyes were really red.

Poor Neville.

November 13th

Mum has a new fad. She is now gluten-free and dairy-free. Watch this space ... THAT won't last!

She is also trying to be healthy by eating lots of what Neville calls "hipster-inspired food." Neville is in a particularly bad mood because Mum sent him to the shop to get her a bunch of stuff that he says is totally the sort of thing that a hipster would buy. He really didn't want to go but Mum kept saying, "Don't be ridiculous, the person on the till will just be scanning the stuff, they aren't remotely interested in what you are buying and most certainly won't be judging you for it."

He came back ranting his head off and saying, "Seriously Jaz - you wanted me to get avocados, chia seeds, couscous, watercress and almond milk.If that isn't a f**king hipster shopping list I really don't know what is .. I might as well have gone in there in a fake beard wearing a bow tie!!! Chia seeds?? F**king chia seeds?? It's the local Co-op for Christ's sake, they hardly know what celery is in there! Do you know how much of a twat I felt asking where the chia seeds were??? Do you?? And do you know where they were? MMMmmmm?? Do you? Nowhere!! That's where they f**king were!!"

I went upstairs to get ready for my dance class but I could still hear him ranting on ... "Bill was in there - I could see him smirking at everything I'd got on the conveyor belt, when I put the almond milk in the bag I wanted to shout, "my wife is intolerant to dairy" across the shop really loudly."

Mum said, "Honestly Neville, he was probably smiling about something else, I don't imagine it had anything to do with you. Anyway, people are a lot more aware these days and they are starting to be much more health conscious. It's not like everyone is in there buying Crispy Creme Donuts and Fray Bentos pies. Anyway, what did Bill buy - just out of interest??"

I heard Neville mutter, "Well actually he had some spinach, a loaf of sourdough bread and a collection of rather nice cheeses."

Mum said "SEE!!" and Neville said, "Well, Fray Bentos pies is hardly likely is it - I don't reckon they even make them anymore. Who'd eat a pie out of a tin in this day and age? Ay?"

As we left for Mum to drop me at dancing, she shouted, "Oh shut up Neville. You really are annoying."

It's true. He is.

November 15th

Auntie Ellie called - she is at something called the United Nations Climate Change Conference in Germany. It sounds like quite a big deal and was something to do with talking about a Paris Agreement. I didn't know what it was, but Mum said it's an agreement where all the countries are working towards combating climate change by cutting out certain gases and creating a sustainable low carbon future for the planet.

Donald Trump has pulled out of the agreement apparently which isn't very good as America is a very big country so it probably produces a lot of gas.

Neville said, "In fairness I produce a lot of gas myself... and so does the dog, perhaps we need a Paris type agreement in this house?" He was making a joke but I actually think that we need SOMETHING - the pair of them are so disgusting sometimes.

November 16th

At school today Izzy decided to make a move with Rob in English. It was going well from what I could see and they were laughing and getting told off by Miss Watt, which is a GOOD sign as they obviously weren't getting work done. Break was straight after English and I caught up to Izzy, I told her how it looked like Rob really liked her and that he was flirting with her a lot but it turned out that Rob was actually flirting with Charlotte because from where I sit I can't tell which girl he is talking to. We took Charlotte to one side to ask her but she says she doesn't like him, but that's totally a huge lie! Like come on, she always hangs around with him, she is non stop taking selfies with him and she always lets him play with her hair. Izzy seemed to believe Charlotte, but me and Em exchanged looks, she thinks the same as me. We decided to give him the death look all day. At lunch he actually realised what we were doing and came over to ask what was going on. Of course Em started explaining and me, Izzy and Alice all shushed her because we weren't going to give in just like that, this meant war! Then the bell went, so we decided that during break time tomorrow Izzy will confront him about Charlotte. Rob still doesn't know exactly what's going on but he'll find out soon enough. I hope I still have time to get a chicken wrap before anything kicks off though. Maybe I'll mention that to Izzy ….

Mum overheard me talking to Em about it and wanted to know what was going on. I told her that Rob was just totally clueless because he didn't get why Izzy is upset. Mum said men get easily confused because women are the superior species and always have been. She said that even the Dalai Lama knows this because he said that "the world is going to be saved by the western woman". Apparently if the Dalai Lama said it, then it's totally true. She hangs on his every word. Well …. him and Oprah Winfrey.

Mum has been very stressed out - she's had a big graphic design job to get done and has been working until all hours. She keeps on about being all out of balance and un-centred, whatever that means. Seems to me she is just tired and needs a few early nights. I heard her telling Neville that the project manager is being aggressive with her and she needs to stand up to him. In order to do this she needs to get her chakras balanced first. Honestly I have no idea what she is on about sometimes. Or what a chakra is. She thinks her throat chakra is blocked and this is stopping her from speaking her "authentic truth" whatever that is. Apparently she's found someone that can do it remotely over the phone. This person is going to send her "healing energy to remove the blockages in her system and realign her body." It's going to cost 150 quid. Honestly, she could be spending that money on me. I suggested she google how to do it instead and then go on the Pretty Little Thing website and get me some stuff to wear at Christmas.

Neville said she must be mad spending that sort of money on some rip off merchant off the internet. Mum got annoyed and told him he didn't understand the energetic connections within the body and how complex it all is. Neville replied that his "beer chakra" was currently out of alignment and stomped off to the pub.

November 17th

Complete drama today. Dan and Jack B were having a stupid play fight and pretending to kick each other in the giblets when Dan tripped and smashed his head on a bench. There was so much blood everywhere. They had to call an ambulance. While we were all standing around not knowing what to do Rob asked Izzy to be his girlfriend. She was supposed to be really angry with him about yesterday but she forgot and said yes.

Dan had 4 stitches in his head. He thinks having a scar is going to make him look cool - he really is an idiot.

November 20th

Just got back from going to Costa with Izzy - she was linking on snapchat with Rob for ages last night but then he just aired her all day today for no reason so she was really upset. When I got home Mum was walking round the garden barefoot with her hands in a prayer position. It's called 'earthing' apparently and it's important to connect with the earth regularly to ground you and keep you at peace. What .. EVER. I personally think it's pretty risky, as it's been a few days since anyone's picked up all the poo in the garden. She's always on about how she doesn't like wearing shoes. When she lived in Australia by the beach she said everyone walked about barefoot and went to the supermarket without shoes on. I can't imagine people here walking around Asda in bare feet - although some people go in there wearing pyjamas. Mum's friend Justin likes Asda because he says it's the only place you can hear people shouting things like "Wayne get your head out that freezer". Mum hates Asda - Neville says it's because she's a snob. She also hates Greggs, and MacDonalds and KFC and service stations. She especially hates service stations that have a Greggs or a MacDonalds in them. She always tries to get Neville to find one with a Waitrose or an M&S Food. That would make some sense if she wanted a superfood salad or something really healthy but she usually ends up with Liquorice Allsorts, Fruit Gums or Percy Pigs.

I know that she wishes she lived somewhere more sunny, especially in winter. I think she gets that SAD thing because she's never as happy in the wintertime. She's got one of those daylight lamp things which she sometimes remembers to put on in the day. When she got it she said it was to provide extra light for taking pictures for her design work but most of the time she just sits in front of it meditating. I get it though, at this time of year I'd LOVE to be somewhere hot where I could swim and get a really good tan.

Me and Em are going to visit Thailand when we are older. Properly though, not like on Miranda, where she goes to the hotel round the corner for a week. Mum keeps going on about there still being small pockets of South East Asia where you can get off the beaten track and have a more authentic experience of the 'real Asia'. She said we'd be better off trying to get to a remote bit of Laos or Burma rather than going to Thailand because it's really commercialised. I told her that we don't want to be off the beaten track, we want to be wherever everyone else is hanging out so we can go to the parties and stuff and meet other backpackers. She walked off shaking her head. Neville said it's something to do with 'The Road Less Travelled' and to take no notice.

We are going backpacking next summer as Mum wants to show me how much fun it is … her version of fun and mine aren't usually very similar but we will see.

November 21st

Izzy sent Rob a message at break to ask him why he was ignoring her. He just ignored her again. She told me she's broken up with him and burst into tears.

November 22nd

Izzy still keeps crying about Rob. I'm so done with it. It's not like they were even a thing for more than like a day.

November 24th

Mum and Neville left me at Grandma's for the weekend as they were going to see their friends in Hampshire and they thought I'd get bored - they were right I'd have been totally bored. They all just drink wine, talk rubbish and want to go to the pub all the time. Before they left the house, Grandma and Grandpa were having an argument about the microwave. It stopped working earlier in the week and Grandma said they needed to get a new one and that Grandpa should measure it so they could go to John Lewis and buy one.

It has to fit in a specific space in the kitchen so Grandma wanted to make sure it was the right size. So Grandpa measured one way in inches and the other way in centimetres!! Grandma got really angry with him saying, "That's completely ridiculous, how will we know what to buy?? Do it properly for goodness sake." Grandpa said, "It doesn't matter woman, a microwave is a nominal module, just like a washing machine or a fridge." Then Grandma replied, "You really are the most irritating person that I've EVER met."

Mum had to push Neville out the front door because he was giggling.

November 25th

Mum texted this morning from Hampshire to say they were having a great time. She said her friend Kathryn was going through a tough patch with her anxiety but Mum was telling her she needed to practice positive thinking because, "thoughts become things" and that Kathryn was feeling much better.

I expect Kathryn just said that to shut Mum up! Ever since she read something called "The Secret" a few months ago she's been going on about positivity and the Law of Attraction and how the energy you send out to The Universe comes back to you - so if you send out good feelings then good things happen to you and if you moan all the time then bad things will happen to you. It all sounded a bit simple to me but she said it's all about scientific principles and the laws of physics and that Einstein proved all this stuff donkey's years ago. I asked Mr Piggot about it in science one day but he said it was a load of New Age nonsense and I should get on with what I was supposed to be doing. I told Mum but she said Mr Piggot is an idiot and someone teaching science in a second rate comprehensive school shouldn't be disputing the findings of one of the worlds most acclaimed geniuses.

Grandma always says, "donkey's years" too. What's a donkey's year? Is that a thing? How is it different to a normal year? Since we were at Grandma's I asked her. Shanequa had just arrived, so as usual, it just turned into a ridiculous conversation.

G: Well I think it means years ago - like back in the old days when people were more dependent on donkeys for things.

S: Seriously Grandma??? I can't even.

G: You can't even what?

S: What do you mean?

G: You said you can't even, you can't even what?

S: What? There isn't a what? What are you on about?

They have quite a few conversations like this.

Shanequa had come over to take me to the cinema to see Paddington 2. It was SO good. Paddington is soooooo cute. I loved it and Grandma gave us a £20 note to get some drinks and some pic'n'mix.

November 28th

Mum had a call from Kathryn's husband to say she wasn't at all well and had been in the hospital overnight with a very nasty panic attack. She's now seeing a special therapist for anxiety and has some strong tablets to take.

So much for Mum and her "positive thinking." Neville said, "See Jaz, I told you your whole 'just think happy thoughts' crap wasn't going to work. You need to stop banging on about that when people have actual health problems!"

December 1st

Ollie came round for dinner. Mum insisted that Neville invite him and Neville has been in a bad mood about it for days. Mum has been looking up vegan websites and food blogs all week in order to make something to impress Ollie. There are a ton of vegetables and spices on the side in the kitchen and she's trying to make cheese out of cashew nuts - it looks like a total disaster!

Neville keeps saying, "We didn't have to invite that twat into the house Jaz - honestly I don't know what you were thinking." And Mum said, "He's your boss Neville, it's only polite that we invite him round and get to know him a bit better. Anyway, it will be nice to find out more about veganism." Neville replied, "Yeah won't that be a bundle of laughs."

I had chicken goujons and oven chips for dinner before Ollie arrived, but I decided to hang about a bit to see what it was about Ollie that Neville found so annoying.

Ollie is actually really good looking and he gets really enthusiastic when he talks about stuff he believes in - like getting rid of plastic and never wearing leather shoes.

Neville was drinking one bottle of beer after another, almost like it was all about to be confiscated and Mum had had too many glasses of wine and was all giggly. Ollie was driving so he only had soda water with lemon in it.

Neville was saying, "You can have one beer and be within the limit." But Ollie said that he doesn't really drink and that he's frankly horrified by the excessive drinking culture we have in the UK. He said that people don't behave like that on the continent and it's no wonder everyone thinks the British are all alcoholics. He also said that the figures relating to the amount of binge drinking done by women over 40 are really quite shocking. I told Ollie that I agreed with him and we both looked at Mum who actually looked a bit embarrassed for once and suddenly asked if anyone wanted some water to go with their drinks (she NEVER does that).

Neville wouldn't let the drinking thing go and kept saying stuff like, "Enjoying a few beers of a night doesn't mean you have any sort of a drinking problem does it?" and, "Surely you can enjoy a glass of something now and again?"

Ollie said that it's all about dependence and people nowadays use drinking as a crutch to deal with stress in their lives. He said there are lots of statistics about parents, and mums in particular, only just about making it through the day because they know they have 'wine o'clock' to look forward to every single night. Mum said, "Well that's not true, I only drink in the week if people are visiting." That made me choke on my squash - she talks SUCH rubbish.

Then Ollie said, "Anyway, it suits me that I don't hang round drinkers all the time, I do loads of running and cross-fit and HiiT exercise so I like to be up early, fully hydrated, with a clear head."

I told Ollie it was very nice to meet him and that I hoped the dinner wasn't too disgusting - I told him it was a bit of a challenge for Mum as she knows nothing about cooking vegan food.

Mum shot me a filthy look, and Ollie turned to her and said, "Speaking of challenges Janice, I've actually just started training for an Iron Man Challenge." And I heard Neville mutter, "Of course you f**king have."

December 2nd

So this morning I asked Mum how the rest of dinner went. She looked a bit green and ill - I thought that was probably all the wine. Turned out it was only partly the wine.

Mum said she asked Ollie why he became a vegan and he told her all about the stuff he'd learnt about farming practices. He went into loads of horrific detail and she had to stop him after he got really graphic describing the slaughter house in the poultry farm he visited. He said that everyone should see these things in order to educate themselves about where their food comes from.

Neville said, "It's all bollocks, all I need to know is that my food comes from Tescos."

Mum said, "It's not that simple though Neville, after hearing all that I won't be eating chicken in a hurry and as for what he said about the farms right before Christmas when they are killing all the turkeys, it's absolutely horrible."

Neville said he was making bacon sandwiches and asked who wanted one. We all said yes, including Mum, which gave him a chance to make fun of her saying, "Oh it's only the poor little chickens and turkeys is it Jaz - you don't care about the all the pig slaughtering then?"

December 3rd

Neville's been off seeing his Dad all day - he took a turn for the worst with his blood pressure but apparently he's feeling a bit better. He was talking about when Neville was a little boy. The nurse said that people can often remember things from a long time ago but can't remember stuff that happened yesterday so that's quite normal.

Neville told Mum it was nice chatting about his childhood, although his Dad did mention him falling on his head quite a lot.

December 10th

It's snowing!!! It's soooooooooo brilliant!! The dog was a bit confused at first but then loved it. She was jumping about getting really excited. So was Neville. We took the sledge out for a bit and then Neville said he'd nip to the shops and get some food. He said, "Who fancies a lovely roast dinner then?" Mum said she wouldn't eat it if he got chicken as she hasn't got Ollie's words out of her head yet.

December 15th

Mum isn't feeling well so she's been even less organised than normal. I actually had to unload the dishwasher yesterday because she didn't do it. She has a really nasty cold and cough and sounds like she is coughing up her insides. She is getting through a million tissues - they are all over the place. She has overtaken the sofa and taken the really snuggly furry throw that I like and is watching endless Christmas films on Netflix. I still have to go to school while she lounges about the place.

Neville said I should be a nicer to her and said, "She really must be ill, your Mother never makes a fuss."

December 16th

Neville has caught Mum's cold - however you'd think he was actually on his deathbed. He keeps moaning and groaning really loudly and asking for Night Nurse and Lemsip. Mum is still not feeling great herself, but she now has to look after Neville. He can just about leave the bed long enough to stagger to the bathroom and back. She said, "He's got Manflu Ruby, the fuss he's making is utterly pathetic. There's a reason it's women who give birth."

I am staying away from the pair of them - I don't want their germs.

Mum said there is a really nasty cough bug thing going around and Debbie's whole family have had it for weeks. Apparently Debbie put on Facebook that she can't remember the last time she didn't have one or other of the kids off of school with some illness or other. It's lucky she is a full-time Mum for her job - she'd need to take every single day off otherwise.

Oh. And the Applebys are going to Lapland (not Lapland UK, ACTUAL Lapland). Mum just watched their dramatic "ticket reveal" video on Facebook and showed it to me. The kids were beside themselves with excitement. They were surrounded by homemade Christmas wreaths and cleverly crafted wooden decorations and about a million fairy lights. Mrs Appleby had baked a plate of Christmas cookies spelling out the word "surprise" and they all had special new Appleby-branded Santa hats to wear.

Mum yelled upstairs to Neville, "The Applebys are going to Lapland," and he replied, "Of course they are, the smug b****rds" before whimpering about needing more Lemsip.

December 18th

Auntie Sophie sent us a video of the little Nativity show they did at Coco's nursery. Coco was dressed as a star and had to sort of dance around on a raised area at the back. We all reckoned she was the best thing in it and Mum said since she can talk really well, she should have had a main part really. The kids playing Mary and Joseph couldn't talk properly AT ALL, so there wasn't much happening for most of the show. Joseph just looked totally confused the ENTIRE time, Mary picked her nose A LOT and one of the wise men cried through the whole thing, because he didn't want to hold his pretend Frankincense parcel. The best part was the Baby Jesus was a bright orange Furby.

Neville said, "That's the most brilliant thing I've seen in ages, that could only have been bettered if one of the shepherds had vomited on the manger."

Mum said, "Well, one of Debbie's kids actually DID vomit on stage during their school nativity performance," and Neville replied, "Well there's a surprise. I assume the full HD video is on Facebook by now?"

December 21st

We finished school today and had a little present swap thing at Costa which was fun. Then we went to Bridget's for Christmas drinks and mince pies. There was loads of nice food for the kids and tons of wine for the parents. They had Christmas songs on so it was really fun and the adults (if you can call them that) were playing beer pong and some other game involving shots and talking in funny voices without showing your teeth. Neville said it's hilarious and it's from a TV show, which it might be, but it makes them all look like demented old people that have lost their dentures. Mum had too much wine and was in a right state! She said it was because she 'forgot to eat.' She NEVER forgets to eat and anyway I saw her have several mince pies!

We walked home which was nice because of all the Christmas lights and seeing how people had decorated their houses. Me and Neville had to keep a close eye on Mum, as she was weaving about the pavement doing what Neville calls her "pinball machine impression." This is some old fashioned arcade game he used to play when he was a kid, where you hit this little ball around a glass covered area to get points and it sort of bounces on and off all the targets in the play area. He said when she is wandering along banging into cars on one side of the pavement then veering across to bang into a garden wall on the other side, it's just like a the ball in the pinball machine - except they make a pinging noise and the things they bash against light up, whereas Mum just sort of mutters and looks surprised when she bangs into something.

It sounded like a weird sort of game, but I googled it and watched a video of an old fashioned pinball game and it made more sense. That's exactly what she looks like.

December 24th

Eeeeek ... I'm excited for presents. I asked Mum if I could have a stocking even though I don't believe in Santa anymore. We are at Grandma's so I've been helping her peel lots of vegetables for tomorrow. We are listening to Michael Buble Christmas songs and chatting. Mum and Neville have gone to the pub with Auntie Sophie and Uncle Marc. They all wedged into Auntie Sophie's car. Mum was fine sitting in the front, but Coco and Felix's car seats are fixed in and can't be moved, so Neville was in the boot and Uncle Marc was sort of pushed in at an awkward angle to lie over the top of the two car seats. When they got to the pub they had to open the back door and pull him out horizontally.

On the way back Neville insisted they swop places so Uncle Marc went in the boot and Neville got pushed in on top of the seats. When they tried to pull him out of the car outside Grandma's house, Uncle Marc insisted he would do it on his own, so he opened the door and proceeded to yank Neville out and drop him on his head. I think he'd had too much beer to feel anything. Then Uncle Marc tried to get back in the car, as he'd spotted a mince pie lying on the floor (left over from the journey up from London) and wanted to eat it. Auntie Sophie wouldn't let him.

December 30th

Christmas was a bit quiet - I got lots of cool presents but everyone was really tired or not feeling well so it wasn't as much fun as normal. Also it's not as much fun because I stopped believing in Santa a few years ago. Coco was really excited though because she still gets all the magic of it, so that was kind of cute.

Mum has still got what Neville is calling her "chicken phobia" and she refused to touch the turkey. Grandma was really annoyed because she'd gone to loads of effort making it all. We all took stuff like snacks and pudding, and canapés and everything but Grandma made the turkey because she likes to do that bit. She kept telling Mum not to be so stupid and saying when they were young they ate whatever they could get their hands on and they were grateful for it.

She said, "We used to eat liver, kidneys, hearts and pigs trotters when we were young - you don't know you're born." I said eating pigs trotters sounded a bit like being on "I'm a Celeb" when they eat all the horrid things in the jungle, but Grandpa said pigs trotters are really tasty.

Neville said, "In my house we used to eat spam out of tins and my Mum used to make corned beef hash once a week." He looked quite nostalgic about it. I looked for corned beef hash on google images. OMG - disgusting! It looks like dog food.

Auntie Eleanor arrived on Boxing Day with a 3-Bird Roast that she'd bought for £130 from a fancy butcher and we all had to do loads more eating (well apart from Mum who just pulled faces and ate a ton of roast potatoes). Neville was making fun of Auntie Ellie saying, "One hundred and thirty quid Ellie? You were done, that butcher's taken you for a right mug. You should have got one of the £9.99 ones from Iceland and given the rest of the money to all those refugees.

Auntie Eleanor said, "Don't be a fool Neville, the 3-Bird Roast from Iceland is simply a bunch of over-processed reconstituted muck. This is all hand-reared, organic meat. It's a world apart from what you are talking about."

And Uncle Dave said, "You know Neville you can actually get one in Aldi for only seven quid - but I reckon that one is a budgie inside a sparrow inside a rat!"

We all spent a lot of time between Christmas and New Year watching TV and going for walks in the cold - the days all got a bit merged into each other.

Oh yeah - meant to say, all my presents were brilliant. Apart from the one from Auntie Eleanor. She got us all toilets!! Seriously. Instead of a present she spent the money on our behalf and donated a whole load of toilets to remote villages in Rwanda that don't have proper sanitation. I'm pleased for the people in the villages but it's not really a present.

December 31st

It's New Year's Eve. It's been really boring. I chatted to Em most of the night - she was in her room because her parents were having a mad party downstairs and they are really annoying when they drink too much (bit like Mum and Neville). Mum is still a bit under the weather and said it's the first time she's not really celebrated New Year's Eve since she was 17. Neville isn't home as Chemical Banana decided that a New Year's Eve gig would be an amazing thing to do.

Mum said Neville put a video on the Chemical Banana Facebook fan page (which doesn't really have any fans) saying the atmosphere was "electric". Mum said the pub looked a bit quiet considering it was New Year. She also said, "When he's all excited tomorrow saying how amazing it was, try and look like you believe him!"

January 2nd

Mum is off on one again. She says it's because of all the "New Year, New You" stuff that is all over social media and in all the magazines. She says it's all anyone can talk about and we all need to stand firm and rally against it. It's just "media indoctrination." I haven't heard anyone talking about it - it must just be people HER age wanting to be new people. She's been rattling about it for hours …so it's certainly all SHE can talk about!! At the moment she is ranting about the evils of the diet industry and about snapchat filters making everyone think their normal skin and faces are not good enough. Neville is on his iPad trying to find something to make for dinner that is fat-free, dairy-free and gluten-free and (according to him) "absolutely bloody taste free" in order to keep her happy. I heard her saying, "I blame the Kardashians" to Neville. It's not their fault she's upset about diet culture. She's upset about it because she's crap at eating healthily and what's left of the clothes she hasn't thrown out are too small for her! She was trying to explain to Grandma how much the "Kardashian Culture" is poisoning the minds of a generation of young women but I don't think Grandma really knew what she was on about, mainly because she asked Shanequa if a Kardashian was some sort of modern cardigan.

- S: Honestly
  Grandma, she's not a cardigan, she's a proper famous person yeah? She's married to Kanye?

- G: Who's he? Does he wear cardigan's too then?

- S: It's got nothing to do with cardigans Grandma, her last name is Kar-dash-ian. Well it was before, but now she's married to Kanye she's called West. But there are lots of them and they are all famous.

- G: Oh ok. No Cardigans. I understand. And what does this Kanye do then - is he a celebrity?

- S: Yeah, like he's a proper famous rapper yeah? He's like mates with Jay-Z and Beyonce and they called their first baby North West.

- Grandpa: (looking up from the crossword) North west??? north west?? Like a compass? What is wrong with these people? It's a bloody nonsense if you ask me ..

- S: Nah it's different yeah? Another one of their kids is called Chicago Grandpa.

- Grandpa: It's like calling a baby Milton Keynes or Leamington Spa. These celebrities are bloody idiots.

January 3rd

So much for rallying against stuff. Mum's joined a gym and signed up to a "30 days to your best body" programme online - Neville said they are both costing "shed loads." Then he said, "Which is properly ironic because she won't." Honestly, they are always telling me I should speak in proper sentences and that didn't even make sense.....

January 4th

Mum dragged me off to Waitrose after school. We never go there as everything costs too much, but Jasmine is popping round tonight and Mum said we need to have posh nibbles in the house and it has to be obvious they are from Waitrose. Honestly she is ridiculous sometimes!

Jasmine wants to talk to Mum about a logo rebrand she needs for her new "Mummy Blog". She said it's just been a "bit of fun" up until now but she's getting so many readers and Instagram followers that she need to "up level" the whole thing. It's all about the challenges of modern parenting in a fast-paced fashion-forward world. Neville keeps laughing and saying, "Challenges?? What f**king challenges are there when you do voluntary work for one hour a week and have staff to do everything for you ????"

So the snacks Mum found in Waitrose are RIDICULOUS. When her friends come round she's happy with Pringles, Skittles and Twiglets .. BUT NO...... just because it's Jasmine she's bought a whole load of weird stuff like pimento stuffed olives with feta; artichoke hearts; pea shoot salad with edible flowers (what even is that?); Manchego cheese and snacking chorizo. She also spent ages hanging around the wine shelf trying to decide what she could buy that would make her look like she knows about wine. In the end she heard some woman say to her friend, "If you can believe it Daphne she actually suggested Sauvignon, and not even ironically, but frankly I think it's hard to go wrong with a pure Cote de Provence Rose." So Mum picked up two bottles of that and tried not to look horrified at the price when it went through the till.

It took FOREVER to get served - the woman in front took AGES!! She was poncing around putting things on different sides of the conveyor belt saying stuff like, "I can't quite recall Rufus, was this for the St Tropez house or for the Sicilly house?" At one point her daughter added something to the trolley and she said, "Honestly Arabella go and put those back, they are essentials carrots, you know I don't buy things from the essentials range, they might not be organic." Then Rufus chimed in saying, "For goodness sake leave her alone Lucy - they're only for the ponies."

While we were putting our stuff through the till, the man behind shouted at his son, "No Orlando I'm not getting you any cashew nuts, you've been an absolute PAIN IN THE ARSE!!" Even the nice lady on the till was struggling to keep a straight face. I actually had to walk out of the shop before Mum had finished paying because I was laughing so much.

It was like watching the Catherine Tait posh people clips on YouTube. I wish we could go there more often - it's hilarious!!

So we get home and even though Mum spent ALL THAT TIME shopping she STILL had to send Neville to the Co-op to pick up some other stuff. I heard her saying, "But I need cocktail sticks Neville.. the label says the pimento stuffed olives have to be served with cocktail sticks."

She deliberately left some of the stuff in the packets and was still putting them into dishes when Jasmine arrived so she could see the Waitrose labels. PATHETIC.

After all the fuss about which wine to buy Jasmine decided she wanted a Gin & Tonic. She talked to Neville as if he was a waiter, which was quite funny, and she was very put out that there weren't any bruised basil leaves available. In the end she settled for cucumber, but didn't look very happy about it. I heard Neville say, "Nice one Jaz, so we are stuck with this overpriced pink shit."

Neville said he'd drop me at netball practice and just as we were leaving, Jasmine was going on about the opportunities that exist for Mumpreneurs (whatever they are) in the online marketplace, and Mum was nodding along like she understood. I heard her say, "Precisely Jasmine, there's never BEEN a better time to be a digital nomad" and Jasmine replying, "I mean totally .. it's like there literally isn't a glass ceiling anymore and you don't even need to leave the house to be super successful."

It's all ridiculous if you ask me - who'd want to read a Mummy Blog? Mums don't do ANYTHING interesting AT ALL!! and as for her ideas about ceilings who'd want one made of glass?? I would hate that - it would feel like there was nothing underneath you and like it could just break any second when you walked on it - and I don't like heights … arghghghghh. I hope some of her other ideas are a bit better than that one …..

January 7th

Jasmine's new and improved "Mummy Blog" is up and running and seems to be attracting a load more interest according to Mum who I think is a bit annoyed about it. She said, "It's all a bit dull if you ask me so goodness knows why so many people are reading it, but at least she's telling people I did the logo and re-brand so I might get some other work from it."

According to Mum the current blog post is part of a series about "difficult parental choices". Mum said, "She's debating whether you should choose skiing or snowboarding when booking your upcoming ski break."

Neville just said, "What upcoming ski break?? Chance'd be a fine thing" and "hardly life and death stuff is it? I can see the headlines now, 'Chaos descends on the UK as parents all over the country despair about their middle class holiday dilemmas' ... what a load of bollocks."

Mum said, "Well we must be in the minority Neville as according to the quotes on the site she is "totally relatable" as a modern day mum blogger. She's being featured in magazines and interviewed for podcasts...."

Mum poured herself a massively large glass of wine and spent the rest of the night curled on the sofa in front of the laptop swearing every now and again.

January 10th

Today would have been Neville's mum's 80th Birthday - he's always a bit sad on her Birthday but he was more sad than normal when he went off to work. He said he'll raise a glass of something for her later.

It's actually been a pretty rubbish day all round. LOADS of people are off school ill. Debbie's entire family have the Novovirus and they are all taking turns to projectile vomit round the house according to Mum. Debbie is not putting too many pictures on Facebook right now, Mum says it's probably because she is too busy washing endless sets of vomit-covered bedding and clothes. Neville said, "If there is ever an unprecedented outbreak of the Ebola Virus in the UK, it will have generated from that woman's house."

All the talk of people being sick was making me feel sick so I went upstairs to do my homework.

January 12th

Mum and "the gang" all went out to the wine bar last night. I heard her crashing around the kitchen trying to make toast at about 11 o'clock. Lizzie went out in a pair of shoes that didn't match. The shoes were both nude with a heel but other than that they didn't look anything alike. None of them noticed. How ridiculous. Too drunk probably. Mum says it's because Lizzie is in quite a new relationship and is all loved up so she isn't thinking about boring day-to-day things.

She started to say, "I remember when me and Neville first got together ..." Good job I was leaving to go to school - I totally DO NOT want to hear about her and Neville being loved up. Disgusting.

I told Em and Izzy. Izzy said, "I don't care how much I was in love, there is no way I would go out in shoes that didn't match - for a start I'd take like a million selfies before I left the house anyway, so SOMEONE would point it out."

Me and Em looked at each other and giggled. Izzy kept asking what was so funny so in the end I told her that in the selfie she posted at break time she had lipstick on her teeth and we decided not to tell her. She stomped off in a sulk and didn't talk to us for the rest of the day.

January 14th

We are just back from a weekend seeing Auntie Sophie in London. We had a great day out yesterday and got some amazing stuff for dinner from Deliveroo. I wish we had that where we live - you can find whatever you like! I had crispy duck pancakes as they are THE BEST!

Neville and Uncle Marc spent most of the afternoon in the pub so me and Mum and Auntie Sophie went shopping with Coco and Felix. Mum usually hates shopping (especially since her thing about commercialisation and being a minimalist) but Auntie Sophie knows some really cool markets and brilliant little shops so Mum actually enjoyed it even though it was really cold, and she even bought a couple of things that she totally doesn't need.

On Sunday morning we went to this really amazing little cafe for brunch. I really liked it as I think I want to be an interior designer so I thought all the exposed brick walls and stainless steel looked really cool. Neville started muttering the minute he spotted a barista with a man bun and asked Uncle Marc whether the man buns or the tattoos bother him more. I don't really think Uncle Marc cares either way but he said "definitely the man buns" to keep Neville happy.

It got worse when we sat down and it turned out you didn't even need to call a waiter, you could order everything at the table via a menu on an iPad. Neville started getting a bit red in the face - that's what he looks like when he's about to have a rant. Mum pointed out that the cafe was actually a cafe slash book shop slash microbrewery so Neville could get himself a hand crafted artisanal beer if he wanted to, instead of getting a cup of tea. That cheered him up no end and him and Uncle Marc started a boring conversation about beer while we decided what to eat. He was a bit happier once he had his beer in his hand but he did have a mini-rant about avocados saying, "When did smashed avocado on toast become a thing - that isn't breakfast! What's wrong with a full English????" Mum started saying that avocados used to be a horrible slimy thing that people filled with vinaigrette dressing as a starter in the 70s and that it was certainly never something you'd eat for breakfast.

Auntie Sophie got a decaf coffee and a babychino for Coco. I got a hot chocolate and Mum ordered a chai latte (that produced a half tut, half sarcastic noise from Neville, who'd just had a go at the barista because he couldn't find anything resembling PG Tips on the iPad). The latte looked so pretty when it turned up, there was this amazing really complicated flower design on the top done with cinnamon powder and a pretty-shaped thing that Mum said is called a star anise. Auntie Sophie says the latte art is really good in this cafe. I got my phone out to Instagram it, as it was soooo cool and that set Neville off again …

"You see - this the problem," he started saying, making pointy stabbing gestures at Mums drink, "That actually is really attractive looking and part of me really wants to take a photo of it. But the fact I'm even thinking that makes me loathe myself."

We stayed for quite a while as Felix was fast asleep. Uncle Marc and Neville had another couple of beers and everyone was having a lovely time. We only left because 3 men came in with extremely long styled beards and Mum knew it would get Neville moaning again. His voice had got really loud because of the beer and he started saying, "I don't get it - really I don't. What's cool about a load of straggly facial hair?? Beards used to be reserved for stinky old maths teachers with leather elbow patches, but SUDDENLY, you can grow a massive ginger beard and you are considered some sort of Greek god." The men were looking over at us so Mum had to push him out the door really quickly.

January 16th

Its soooooooooo cold. I really hate it.

Neville is moaning about the fact that everyone is sharing photos of the dials in their cars that show how cold it is. He just keeps saying "It's f**king freezing, we know it's f**king freezing, I don't need to look at hundreds of pictures of temperature gauges to know it's f**king freezing."

Coco has caught a nasty winter bug at nursery so her and Felix aren't well at all. Poor Auntie Sophie - she sounded worn out when Mum was talking to her. Uncle Marc was sick too, but Auntie Sophie said that was nothing to do with winter bugs and a lot to do with his old friends from university and someone's very large whiskey collection.

January 20th

Neville sent a text to me that was obviously intended for Mum. It said:

FFS That TWAT Ollie is sharing a map of every f**king run he does (little man running emoji). Like I give a crap (poo emojji)

When he got in from work I told him he'd sent it to me, not Mum, and said I thought if someone has set themselves a big challenge and wants to share how they are getting on, then their friends should encourage them and be happy for them.

Neville just said, "A - I'm not his friend, and B - it was bad enough I had to hear about every run he did and how fast it was. NOW I have to see the actual bloody route on the map? Bloke's a right TWAT."

Mum started to say, "Well if you are not prepared to be supportive of his fitness journey …."

Neville replied, "Journey? Why is everything a f**king journey these days? People just used to go to the gym and not go on about it - now it's a f**king JOURNEY ? Same with bloody illnesses - people used to get cancer - now they go on a cancer journey. It's not a bloody journey, it's a shitty disease FFS. If I ever get cancer and someone refers to it as a journey, I will bloody well punch them in the face."

Mum said Neville should unfollow Ollie if it bothers him so much. Haha - that's a joke coming from her - she hasn't done that with Jasmine or Debbie!

She added, "Removing toxic people from your life is an act of self-care."

Neville said, "Haven't you got a mug with that written on Jaz - or is it a t-shirt? I'm sure I've seen that somewhere."

Mum said, "Piss off Neville, you don't understand me."

I think she should get THAT printed on a t-shirt instead.

January 24th

Auntie Ellie FaceTimed - she is at the annual meeting of some big important Economic Forum in Switzerland. She's decided to pop over to see us when it's finished in a couple of days. Someone she works with gave her 2 tickets to see Hamilton in London. Mum's a bit jealous as she'd like to see it, but Auntie Ellie is taking an old friend of hers instead.

Neville said, "Ellie on another plane is she? I thought she was all about saving the planet? Her carbon bloody footprint is a right joke."

January 26th

Today was so cool - we finally got to go to the cinema to see The Greatest Showman - I must be like the LAST person in the WHOLE WORLD to see it since it came out on Boxing Day! I know all the songs by heart and I wanted to go for ages. Mum took me and Em as a treat - we usually wait for the DVD to come out. We had to stop at Tescos first to get sweets as Mum always complains that the pick n' mix costs an "arm and a leg." I told her that it's a really stupid expression — she said, "It's not as stupid as saying BAE" - I don't even say that, she's SO annoying. Anyway, because of the Tescos thing we got there late and ended up walking in in front of loads of people. It didn't really matter as there were still loads and loads of adverts. Turns out Joe Baines from 8LB was in there with his Mum, but we pretended not to see him. I used to really like him when I was younger - NO IDEA why!!

It's such a good film - but it was a total nightmare because Mum kept singing along which was pretty embarrassing because her voice is terrible. And then when "This is Me" came on she sung really really loud and even stood up with her arms stretched towards the ceiling near the end of the song - thank goodness we were near the back and the room was so dark. Even so, people were turning round and staring so me and Em just slunk down in our seats and hid behind our coats. OMG I really hope Joe Baines didn't figure out that she's with us. Soooooo embarrassing!!!! When we left the cinema I told Mum she shouldn't have done that, but she just made some big ranting speech about it being "an empowering anthem for women everywhere", and that "we should all accept ourselves exactly as we are." She said it's about "fighting back against the unrealistic pressures that society puts on women to look a certain way and realising true beauty comes from within."

Then she said she just needed to pop to Boots quickly because she'd run out of anti-wrinkle cream and those tights that really hold her stomach in.

January 27th

Went to Grandma's for lunch so we could all catch up with Auntie Ellie on her flying visit. She'd arrived back from her conference and gone straight to London yesterday to see Hamilton. She said Hamilton was excellent. Mum tried to tell her how good The Greatest Showman was but Auntie Ellie said she doesn't have time for that sort of trivial rubbish when humans are singlehandedly destroying the planet with their irresponsible behaviour. I don't know why she has time for one show and not for another, but what do I know? She did bring us tons of fabulous Swiss chocolate though so I didn't say anything.

The meeting thing she had just been to was huge and very serious sounding. All the famous world leaders were there - The nice Canadian one, Trump (yuk), Macron, the German woman, the Prime Minister of India and our ridiculous PM Theresa May. Everyone says that she is a bit like a robot because she doesn't show any emotion and so lots of people call her "The Maybot" instead of her proper name.

Auntie Eleanor got Grandma a bit confused while she was talking about the conference.

- AE: It was pretty inspiring stuff and actually it was pretty unprecedented, the entire panel were female. Not the usual "Manel."

- G: Mammals? Why were they talking about mammals - wasn't it about economics? I thought that's what you did?

- AE: Well, yes I do. But no - I'm talking about a "Manel" - M-A-N-E-L - as in a "MALE panel" - you usually STILL get the panel entirely made of up of men. Even now. But this year we had a full female panel. It was excellent and not before time.

I asked her if she talked to Trump and she said, "Good god NO, I couldn't bear to even look at the man."

Then Shanequa said, "Well, did you like properly meet ANY of the famouses then Auntie?" and Auntie Ellie said that she met Malala who was there talking about education for girls.' Shanequa said, "Who? I am supposed to know who she is?" I said I knew who she was, because we learnt about her in PSE. She was given a Nobel Peace Prize and she got shot in the head because she wanted to go to school.

Auntie Ellie said, "Yes Ruby that's correct." And she added, "Ella, she is utterly inspiring. That's the sort of role model you young girls should be looking up to, not these godforsaken excuses for human beings like the Kardashians."

Grandma was really pleased, because she was able to say she knew all about the Kardiashians and their offspring. She said, "I totally agree with you Eleanor - no one should be worshipping anyone that takes their clothes off all the time on the interwebs and calls their child South East."

Shanequa said, "It's North West" and Grandma said, "What is?" and Shanequa said, "Never mind" and rolled her eyes at me.

On the way home Neville said, "So Eleanor is still a raging feminist then." Mum said, "No she isn't Neville, she just believes in equality for the sexes that's all, and she likes to speak her mind."

He said, "Well you say that Jaz, but a couple of strong vodkas and she'll be burning her bra and ranting about smashing the patriarchy - you know what she's like. I'm amazed she managed to be in the same room as Trump frankly without giving him a piece of her mind. No wonder she's still single."

Mum said, "Don't be stupid Neville - she's single out of choice because she's too busy to be in a relationship unless she can find an intellectual equal. And people don't burn their bras anymore …. have you seen the price of a decent bra ??"

January 28th

The "fashion" element of Jasmine's blog has featured a post on "Which jeans are a 'must have' for the busy multi-hyphenate mum." Neville said, "What the bleeding hell is a multi-hyphenate Mum?"

Mum said, "It's when people do a bunch of jobs - you know like "actor-singer-dancer.""

Neville said, "So she's a what? Irritating twat-kept woman-writer of b*llocks?"

Mum said, "Oh shut up - that's not the point of the blog - although according to this, she's apparently a writer-blogger-social media influencer! Anyway the blog is about which are the best jeans to wear to suit her "hectic" lifestyle. It's completely insane - do you know, the cheapest pair she recommends are £125!! They go up to about £450 - for a pair of JEANS!! And that's not the worst part. She's been given her favourite pair FREE from the company as a thank you for promoting them! They've sold out since she put them on her blog. There are thousands and thousands of people reading it Neville - it's ...it's...... "

She was struggling for words so Neville chimed in, "It's a pile of utter shite is what it is Jaz."

January 29th

I've started to go to a Zumba class with some of my friends - it's really FUN!

We were all having dinner after I got back from the first class and I said to Mum that she should come along as there are lots of women there that are as old as she is. Neville laughed so hard he snorted beer all over his pork chops. Then he said, "I wouldn't bank on it Ruby, she might be the same age as some of them, but trust me, your mother has the co-ordination of a newborn foal that's just fallen out of its mother's whatsit."

Mum was really pissed off with him and said she was going to have a candlelit bath and get some important "me time". Neville said "oh yeah here we go, f**king "me time". I'll wash up again then shall I Jaz?? God forbid you miss out on "me time", the f**king world will end."

Mum told him to shut up and said that "self-care is absolutely vital to maintain good self-esteem, high levels of confidence and optimum body health." So Neville shouted up the stairs, "Yeah right, your body is a temple and all that shit. Well I tell you what Jaz, if it IS INFACT a f**king temple, then it must be constructed entirely out of Haribos and cheese."

Mum shouted back, "Oh hilarious! You just don't understand. It's really important that I relax and rejuvenate properly Neville!!!! You just don't get it, there are lots of complexities involved in raising a teenager and you are at work most of the time - thank goodness for the gang being there for me. It takes a village you know!"

Then Neville just muttered, "Yeah don't think I don't know anything about f**king villages" and stomped off to play Clash of Clans.

I thought about doing the washing up to be helpful, but realised that I haven't texted Em back which is waaaay more important. One of them will wash up later anyway, so I'm sure they won't mind.

January 30th

Mum is constantly singing stuff from the Greatest Showman soundtrack around the house. Neville says she sounds like a cat that is being strangled very, very slowly … I kind of agree with him. It's actually sort of ruined the whole thing for me….. Mum says it doesn't matter if she can't sing well - it's all about self-expression and doing things that "light you up" even if you aren't the best at them. She says "women are tainted by the curse of perfectionism and this stops them from living in authenticity and doing things purely for fun."

Neville said, "It's not about you singing perfectly Jaz, it's about the fact that WHEN you sing, I want to poke really, really sharp hot things right into my eyeballs."

Mum replied, "I'm starting to think that you really don't understand me Neville," and disappeared off to have another long bath. This seems to be her answer to everything these days. Neville looked at me and said "Understand her??? Of course I don't bloody well understand her …." I said that I don't understand her either most of the time and the two of us decided to watch a couple of old episodes of Outnumbered and eat some toasted crumpets.

January 31st

Mum is pissed off with Neville (there's a surprise).He has developed what Mum calls "gaming tourettes" and is spending hours playing Clash of Clans. He says every time he tries to upgrade anything in his village it takes about 19 hours and he keeps being attacked whilst he's logged off by someone called "Muktar the Mighty" who smashes his village and steals his gold. Neville is walking around the house muttering, "That little shit Muktar is my Nemesis."

I expect Neville is as rubbish at playing Clash of Clans as he is at performing with Chemical Banana.

February 5th

It's Neville's Birthday - I've got him a personalised T-shirt off of the internet that says "Team Muktar" on the front. Me and Mum think it's hilarious. Neville is going to hate it!

Uncle John FaceTimed to say Happy Birthday to Neville. We tried to say hello to Chad and Brad but Brad was chasing Chad around in the background threatening him with a baseball bat. Auntie Ellie was trying to FaceTime us too, so I showed Mum how to do like a conference call so we could all talk. Auntie Ellie said, "What on earth are those boys doing?" Uncle John laughed and said, "Just a bit of fun with the baseball bats Ellie." Then he shouted, "Go on Brad, smack him one."

She said, "It's not funny John, you shouldn't be encouraging them to be violent towards each other."

He said, "They are fine. Chad smacked Brad over the head with his skateboard last week. There doesn't seem to be any lasting damage." Then he added, "Still... if there is any damage it will save me a ton of money in college fees."

Neville said he was popping to the pub for a couple. He was gone for hours. Mum had made him a nice Birthday dinner but it was all dried up by the time he got back. She said she's not bothering again.

I'd gone to bed by the time he opened his gifts but he did send me a text saying "nice one Ruby" and a photo of him wearing the t-shirt. I think he only liked it because he'd had so much beer.

February 7th

Jasmine has released another blog in the "difficult parental choices" series.

Neville is beside himself. She is talking about the fact that it's essential to get her 8 year old a new phone and should she be going for the IphoneX or is there a decent Android equivalent. Given that he also has a MacBook Air and an iPad, will compatibility be an issue?

Neville said, "A thousand pound phone? For an 8 year old? A f**king 8 year old. Well I've heard it all now."

Mum said, "She is asking for people's opinions on the subject." And Neville said, "I'll give her a f***king opinion!"

Mum said she knew Neville would rant about the blog post - he was already in a bad mood because loads of Muktar's friends have been ganging up on him and attacking his village.

I noticed he's not worn the t-shirt again. I don't care. I enjoyed annoying him with it. It's about time I annoyed him, he's always annoying me.

February 10th

Mum is really miserable because it's so cold every single day. She hates it and sort of goes into hibernation. Wish I could do that, but I have to go to school. It's horrible in the morning and she won't even give me a lift because she has to scrape the ice off of the car so I have to walk to school freezing to death. It's not fair at all.

And I've fallen out with Izzy (or rather she's fallen out with me). It was because I turned up to a party in the same outfit as her. I didn't even know she had the same outfit - she normally tries on all her new clothes and videos herself in them and then puts a bunch of them on Insta asking for everyone's opinions. It's not like I did it on purpose but she still isn't talking to me. Best bit was she had it on back to front!!! Sooo funny. The zip is supposed to be at the back.

Mum just said to ignore her and that "real friends don't carry on like that" which isn't particularly helpful! She also said that you need to "protect the vibrations around you and remove people from your circle if they are bringing toxic energy into your life." Izzy will come round in a couple of days and come back like nothing happened - like normal.

Neville just said, "Threw her toys out the pram again, did she? Tell her to stop being an idiot." Then he added, "There was none of this rubbish when I was younger. That's the difference between men and women you see Ruby, lads just punch each other and it's all sorted in no time."

I told him that wasn't helpful either, as I wasn't about to start punching my friends. If that's how he carried on with his friends when he was young it kind of explains his wonky nose.

February 11th

Auntie Ellie face timed Mum in a right strop. She said she's sick of people thinking she is "lesser than" because she has chosen her career above relationships or motherhood. I didn't really understand and asked Mum "lesser than what?" but she kind of waved me away and carried on rambling to Auntie Ellie about how women should be "lifting one another up, not putting one another down."

Auntie Ellie said, "This is serious Janice, don't quote one of your inspirational memes at me. It's quite possible I'm being passed over for promotion because I don't fit neatly into a "married with 2.4 kids" box." Mum said that's she's sure that isn't the case at all and that people surely respect the choice of the individual a bit more nowadays. Auntie Ellie said, "You would like to bloody well think so in 2018, but it looks like Mary is more likely to get the position - it's not even as if she sees her bloody kids, they are all at private boarding school. Hardly an earth mother."

Oh and my Art teacher is leaving - she's really nice, it's so annoying. Why can't the really useless teachers leave?? Neville said,

"Don't worry, they probably will. Teachers are being taken for right mugs by the government Ruby, you wait, loads of them will be chucking it in before too long you mark my words."

February 14th

It's Valentine's Day today. Some people at school got cards but I didn't get any. I don't really care since there isn't anyone I like at the moment. Well that isn't really entirely true. There is someone that I really, really, REALLY like but it's pointless. He totally doesn't even know that I exist! Izzy got a card from Dan but she put it in the bin.

Neville bought Mum some flowers which I thought was quite sweet of him but Mum told him that she doesn't like enforced holidays and it would be much more meaningful if he bought her flowers randomly on another day, instead of when "society" told him he was supposed to be romantic. Poor Neville, he does try. Even if they WERE tatty looking ones from the petrol station.

Truth is I think Mum's upset because Jasmine's husband whisked her away to a 5 star hotel in London called The Ned. There are photos of her sitting on a massive 4 poster bed in something called a Terrace Suite with a bucket of champagne and roses all over the bed. It looks like one of those American rom com films. They have a private terrace. The website says the room is £900 a night - I looked!! Turns out they got an upgrade from the manager because Jasmine said she'd do a little review on Instagram and her blog. It's sooooooo fancy!

Mum said the whole thing looked like a complete cliche but I could tell she was a bit teary. To cap it all Jasmine added that the manager had given her a free spa treatment on top of getting the most expensive room! Me and Mum looked it up - the Spa has "Elixir" treatments with vitamins and collagen and stuff and they hook you up to a drip a bit like on Casualty. The one Jasmine is getting is a "supercharged antioxidant hit" that rejuvenates and hydrates. It WOULD cost £350 if she was ACTUALLY paying. She also put on her Instagram that she's been invited back in summer, with a FREE suite, to try out the roof top pool.

Neville said, "I know Jaz, how about I whisk you off to the nearest Travelodge, chuck some petals on the bed, get you a nice Greggs pasty and hook you up to a bag of Gin?" I know he was joking and trying to cheer her up, but he made it even worse and she actually burst into tears saying something about hormones and lack of sleep.

I told Neville to go and get her a bottle of Prosecco and a Curly Wurly from Sainsbury's then make himself scarce playing Xbox or Clans for the night. I found a really nice film on Netflix that was actually called "Valentine's Day" so me and Mum watched that with a snuggly blanket, we both cried at the sad bits (and the cute bits) and she cheered up a bit.

February 15th

Found out yesterday in America a student shot and killed 17 kids in a school in Florida and injured lots more. It happens all the time over there - feels like almost every couple of weeks there is something on the news about a school shooting. It's soooooo scary - but I think they are so used to it now they don't really think about it. I really worry about my cousins living there. I'd HATE to go to school thinking that some crazy person might suddenly turn up and shoot people. It sounds like something from a film but it happens ALL THE TIME! I was asking Neville why they don't do something about it and make it a safer place. He said that people there are pretty determined to keep their guns so nothing will ever change.

Then he said, "Whatever you do don't get your mother or Eleanor on the subject of gun control - it gets really out of hand". I went on snapchat to talk to Jaime about it. She agrees with me that they need proper gun control. She said something needs to change and maybe her generation will be the ones that do it.

February 16th

It's been half term and it's been really really boring because it's been so cold and miserable. Mum's been working a lot so I've been trying to keep myself entertained.

Debbie's family had a disastrous holiday to Lanzarote where all the kids got ear infections from the hotel pool and the insurance are being difficult about paying the doctor's bills.

February 19th

Jasmine's blog is all about the difficulties of keeping children fully entertained with educational games and crafts during school holidays. Mum says that's rich since they are currently away on their "middle class skiing slash snowboarding holiday" and the kids are probably in ski-school and with babysitters all day.

Neville said, "What is this tripe? You'd think she was the first person to have ever given birth and raise humans, whilst holding down a job at the same time. Oh yeah - I forgot, it's her husband who holds down the job whilst she writes this sanctimonious bullshit."

February 21st

Nothing has really been going on - it's cold, everyone is fed up and school is rubbish. I can't really be bothered to write much at the moment.

Neville had an interview for a new job at his company but they wanted him to do more work for the same money so he said he told them "to piss off and stick it where the sun doesn't shine"... whatever that means. I bet he didn't tell them to piss off at all. He always makes stuff up. It really didn't help that Ollie got a massive bonus. There was a LOT of swearing.

Feb 23rd

It's absolutely freezing and something called "The Beast from The East" is coming and bringing loads of snow - we are going to have the worst weather in a really long time so it says on the internet. Neville is ranting about the heating bill and the fact that everything will "come to a standstill" and Mum is ranting about the fact that "this country really can't handle any sort of weather." They are both going on about the fact that in places like Canada they get a tough winter every year and it's fine, and in England we get half an inch of snow and all the schools shut.

I hope school does shut - that would be cool.

Neville says at least the Daily Mail will be pleased - they predict the worse winter weather in a century every single year and it never happens.

Feb 24th

We went to Grandma's for lunch as it was Auntie Sally's birthday. Mum was ranting on about Jasmine's blog so me and Shanequa were trying to explain to Grandpa what influencers are.

Shanequa said, "I don't know about this like Mum blog thing, 'cos like that woman is well old. But it's a thing yeah? You like talk about stuff that you like and people give you like free stuff and money and that."

Grandpa said, "So you get paid just for talking about things?"

S: Totally. It's like YouTubers yeah? They do their videos and like ... get money. It's a proper job yeah?

G: Well, I'd hardly call it a job. Who gives them money just to make films about rubbish?

Auntie Sophie started to explain about how they make content and they vlog and get followers and then the money comes from the ads around the vlogging. Grandpa just kept insisting it was nonsense.

He was seriously struggling enough with the idea of people vlogging to make money, but Uncle Marc started telling him about unboxing. It was SO FUNNY!

G: What do you mean they just take things out of boxes? Why?

UM: Well they unpack them and talk about the products and then people that follow them are likely to buy the products.

G: So you film yourself taking something out of a box and that makes you money? The world's gone mad! What happened to bloody grafting for a living? In my day we came home exhausted, we knew what hard work really was.

S: Well I reckon YouTubers work like really hard. You gotta be like on it ALL THE TIME and like looking really good yeah? Like you gotta put make-up on every day, and go loads of gym classes and stuff? Like you are TOTALLY in the public eye yeah? It's like you literally can't go out looking rough 'cos randoms are gonna want selfies with you and that?

Grandpa got really angry and snapped, "Oh for goodness sake, that's not WORK Ella. Honestly, it's utter bloody nonsense if you ask me."

Feb 27th & 28th

YAAAAASSSSSS! It snowed. And they shut the school for 2 whole days. It was brilliant - we all went sledging over the fields - it was really good fun. We took the idiot dog out too but the snow is really, really deep in places and her legs are really short so she got sort of half buried and couldn't really run through it properly.

February 29th

To be honest I'm totally bored with all the snow now. It was alright for like a day.

March 3rd

Mum and Neville are going to someone's 60th birthday party - 60! That's like totally ancient! Apparently he has built himself a MASSIVE man cave thing in the garden - it's big enough to have a proper bar and a pool table in it. It's his 60th present to himself. Neville is really jealous. I'm just really annoyed - it's made Mum and Neville start the "shed" arguments all over again. Uncle Dave calls it "Shed-gate" and says they aren't allowed to talk about it when he is there. That name doesn't really make sense though, because they are happy with the gate we've got, but I totally agree on banning them from talking about it.

I'm going for a sleepover to Alice's tonight. Em is going and two other girls from Alice's netball team that I don't really know but I've met them before and they are really nice.

March 4th

Mum and Neville both have hangovers and don't seem to be speaking to each other. Goodness knows what went on last night. I wouldn't be surprised if it was something to do with that bloke's amazing shed. I think Neville must have been a right pain because he is trying really hard to be nice to Mum today and keeps saying stuff like, "Do you want some tea Jaz?" or "Can I get you a sandwich." And Mum is really stoney-faced but trying to be polite saying stuff like, "No thank you very much Neville" or "No I'm FINE" over and over.

I can't be bothered to find out what the matter is. They will sort it out. Probably.

I decided to FaceTime Izzy and tell her about the sleepover. I had a BRILLIANT time. We did all these really hilarious recreations of Vines that were so funny. I fell asleep first and the girls drew on my face with eyeliner and piled a load of bags of crisps on my head and took photos. That always happens - I can't stay awake until really late like everyone else. Izzy didn't want to talk about it. I think she was annoyed that she wasn't invited - she always ignores Alice though so I don't know what she expected.

Apparently a bloke who used to be a spy and his daughter got poisoned today in Salisbury and people think it might have been done by some Russians. They were on a bench at the time. Mum says her friends don't live very far away from there and she should ring and check they are all OK.

March 11th

Yesterday was Mum's birthday so we went to Cambridge for the weekend. It was quite cool - we stayed in a cute Airbnb and went punting on the river. We saw all the posh university buildings and everything and there was a man in a bin playing a guitar. Apparently he's quite famous.

We had some nice meals, went to a proper old sweet shop and saw all the students cycling about. It's a nice place.

There were students sitting by the river drinking bottles of Champagne. Mum said it wasn't like that when she was a student. She said they drank pints of cider for a pound in plastic glasses.

We went to this really old pub with lovely little rooms and comfy chairs in it. It was nice and snug and the fire was on so we stayed for a bit while Mum and Neville drank lots of wine. They were talking about some hotel in Dublin that they stayed in when we all got trapped in Ireland because of a volcanic ash cloud. It was a pretty boring conversation and I don't remember going to Ireland because I was really small at the time, so I ignored them and just played on my phone.

The pub had a sign outside saying "Come in and enjoy the worst pie that one woman on Trip Advisor has ever had in her whole life." I thought that was funny and Neville took a photo of it for Instagram.

I think Mum enjoyed her birthday - but she isn't happy about getting older. I don't get it - I LOVE birthdays. She is going out with the girls this week to celebrate so that should cheer her up!

March 12th

Jasmine is sharing images of different rooms in her house on Instagram and on her Blog. It's sooooooo GORGEOUS. I've never been to her house because I'm not friends with Chloe AT ALL, so I had no idea how big it is, or how nicely decorated. Chloe hangs out with a whole bunch of people in my year that I CAN'T STAND so I've never even been for a party! Every room looks totally amazing -

Jasmine just has the best taste. All the furnishings are so lovely - amazing cushions and throws and fabulous lights, everything is completely colour toned … it's stunning. I haven't told Mum, but I have a secret Pinterest account because I like interior decorating. Now TONS of the pins are from Jasmine's blog and that would really piss Mum off!

Also, I feel a bit embarrassed to think she came to our house - she must have thought it was a right state!! None of the furniture matches, it's all just tatty old bits and pieces, loads of the cushions clash and half the house needs repainting. I'd love to live in a house like Jasmine's. Mum says we shouldn't think like that, because it's "sending the wrong messages to The Universe" and it means we aren't grateful for what we have and will end up feeling worse. She calls it "compare and despair".She heard some mindset coach talking about ways to deal with it on someone's Insta stories and said it was very helpful. What wasn't helpful was that she couldn't remember which coach it was.

March 13th

Mum is complaining that Louise (the woman from school) is at an exclusive resort in Costa Rica hosting a "Wellness Retreat." She keeps saying, "She was really dull at school, how come she's a wellness expert with a ton of followers, swanning around all the exotic places the world. I was more popular than her in school." So much for stopping "compare and despair." That lasted a whole day!

The Prime Minister said she thinks the Russians poisoned the people on the bench. Mum's friends are all fine but they said that the bench was quite near to Sainsbury's and people aren't very keen to shop there at the moment. Some important looking men took the bench away to be examined a few days ago.

Neville keeps on about someone called Putin being behind the whole thing - along with Brexit. I heard him saying, "They are funding the far right Janice and fuelling all this hate, you mark my words."

I don't know what Brexit has to do with benches in Salisbury but I'm pretty sure Neville is NOT an expert on politics. I am sooooo bored of it. It doesn't really matter what you are talking about these days, whatever it is, it's because of Brexit. I don't really understand Brexit, I know it's got something to do with Europe, but it sounds really boring and I'm pretty sure whatever it is, it can't be responsible for EVERY single disaster in the world.

March 14th

Jaime took part in this big country wide protest against guns in America. There were loads and loads of people there and lots of young people like her. She put some brilliant pictures on Instagram. She had a big sign saying, "Thoughts and prayers won't save lives, but gun control will."

I thought that was clever.

She put some of the photos on the family WhatsApp. Mum said, "Nice one Jaime, well done taking for taking action", and Auntie

Ellie said, "I'm very proud of you Jaime, it's up to your generation to make fundamental change." Shanequa wrote, "Dope. You are like so WOKE !!!" so then Grandma wrote, "Are they smoking cannabis????" and Shanequa wrote, "Wot??? It's like you literally don't get me Grandma."

Then I had to explain that dope sort of means awesome - but Grandma said, "Why can't she just say that then?"

March 15th

It's freezing again and the "Beast from the East" is supposed to be coming back again this weekend. Mum's annoyed with Neville. She had her hair cut and highlighted on Monday and he STILL hasn't noticed. Even though she stood in front of him all dressed up before going out with the girls and said, "How do I look?" he just said, "Yeah Jaz" and went back to doing something on his phone.

March 16th

Mum went out last night for her second birthday celebration. She said she managed to smack straight into a tree whilst walking the dog this morning. She said it was because she wasn't paying attention but I bet she was hungover.

At supper time, Mum was telling Neville all about her evening. They went to the local wine bar. Jane realised when she got home the size tag had been hanging out the back of her new jeans all night. The service was really slow so Katie went behind the bar and started to sort the drinks out, shouting, "Right, what are we 'aving?" The doorman said if she did it again she'd be thrown out. Lizzie is worried that her daughter is copying her habits too much. She said her daughter was playing a little game of shops yesterday and left a note in the shop saying, "Popped out for wine, back in 5 minutes". She's also started asking "is it wine o'clock yet" like it's a real time.

Mum said, "I don't think Lizzie should worry, it's just because wine o'clock is the same time as dinner time, so she's worked out that's when she gets fed."

Apparently, Bridget said her girls never played tea parties or picnics when they were little, they played parties with pink fizzy drinks in cocktail glasses and sometimes they played "hangovers" as well.

Mum said, "It's all just a bit of fun isn't it? It's not like any of us drink that much."

Seriously!??!??

March 18th

We all went to the pub for Sunday lunch - it was really snowy again because "The Beast" came back, but wasn't as bad as the last time or as bad as they said it would be. They called it a mini-beast on the news. That reminded me of when I was really small and we used to have to dress up when we were studying certain things. Mum dressed me up as a ladybird for mini-beast day. I look a bit scared in the photo, but it's a cool outfit considering she made it herself and didn't order it off of Amazon.

It made me think of when I was in infant's school and I thought INSET days at school were actually called "Insect" days and I thought that the teachers all had to go into school dressed as insects. It's quite cute really. I also used to see a lorry around town called The Poo Lorry. Neville always said it did "exactly what it says" and was a lorry that dealt with poo. I used to laugh when I saw it and asked Neville one day whether the man that drove The Poo Lorry had to go to work dressed as a poo. Neville said, "I reckon his job is shit enough, excuse the pun, so making the poor sod dress up as a massive turd seems a step too far."

Lunch in the pub was really yummy and they had a lovely big fire lit. Bridget and Helen and their families came too. We actually had a really good time, but on the way home Mark and Neville drew giblets on the windscreens of people's frosty cars.

They are SO embarrassing. I think they are actually worse than the boys in my class.

March 21st

Ant from Ant & Dec was arrested for drink driving. That's a bit sad. The papers said he is going into rehab.

Mum's friend Jane put a photo of her and her kids walking a dog on WhatsApp - the kids are obsessed with dogs but Jane doesn't want one so they are doing "Borrow my Doggy" on the internet. The dog looks really cute - Helen asked what it is - apparently it's a little Cockapoo. Helen said she though it looked like a Shih Tzu/Poodle cross, like her dog. It's supposed to be called a Shihpoo - but Helen calls it a Poo Shit !

That's like a friend of Neville's that got a Jack Russell crossed with a Poodle. They are called Jackapoos, but her son thought it should be called a "Poo Russell" - Neville thought that sounded a bit like an order, well…. if you happen to be called Russell it does.

Anyway - they said Borrow my Doggy is great - I said they could have borrowed the Idiot from us, but Neville thought "Borrow My Idiot" wouldn't catch on so well as a business.

Mum is being soooo annoying. Magda is coming tomorrow so she is yelling at me and Neville about tidying up and cleaning the house. Honestly what's the point in having a cleaner if you are going to clean before she comes?   I like it when she's been though. My bed looks like it's in a hotel and she folds the end of the toilet paper into a point.

March 26th

OMG - so today right before dinner Neville was scrolling through the news on his phone and he said, "Listen to this Jaz - today in America they performed the first ever penis and scrotum transplant on an injured soldier - how amazing is that."

Why does Neville have to talk about giblets?? Especially just before we are about to eat. AND especially when we are about to have sausage and mash. Honestly. The absolutely worst part about it is that Neville and Mum always find stuff like this funny.

Adults are all the same - I remember a few years back when Ella was still called Ella we were all on holiday and she had a melon that was sort of a double melon and Grandpa said, "Oh look Ella, your melon looks like a scrotum." DISGUSTING! Shanequa still doesn't really like melons because of that.

March 27th

Easter holidays. YAAAASSSS. It's sooooooo great not to be at school. Loads of people are on holiday, but some haven't left yet so Me, Em, Izzy and Alice went shopping today in Waterfield Lakes shopping centre. We were having a great time, we had been shopping and had McDonalds but the time had flown by and we had to get back to meet Mum in the car park by Costa. We also had to bin the McDonalds wrappers to avoid a lecture!! We were in M&S buying Percy Pigs and Colin Caterpillars … M&S is like at the exact opposite end. There was this really slow old woman and we were trying to hurry her a little because we were already late, once we had paid we all legged it through the massive shopping centre past loads of slow dawdling people who all, btw, gave us the weirdest, dirtiest looks as if we were invading their personal space, we didn't even touch anyone!!!! Alice dropped everything because her bag broke and that held us up even more, Mum was waiting in the car and she phoned me and sounded very angry so I screamed at them to get a move on. We sprinted past like a million more shops before finally getting to Costa about 10 minutes later. We were catching our breaths as we calmly walked through. Once we got to the car park I spotted Mum's car. Right that moment it started pouring with rain. We ran to the car and I was expecting her to be super angry and waiting impatiently to drive off... but she was sitting in the driver's seat with her legs crossed and eyes closed, meditating. In the middle of a public space just...MEDITATING. She's so embarrassing!!

Of course at that very moment Jake Lakson walked past, with Rob too. They saw my mum and burst out laughing because stupid whale songs were on full volume and she had all the windows open in the pouring rain. Btw Jake Lakson is the FITTEST boy in my year and I have the BIGGEST crush on him, now he thinks I'm a complete weirdo with a mentally disturbed mother !!! I think I preferred it when he didn't know who I was. I was trying to get Mum's attention because it was chucking it down and we were getting soaked but the music was really loud. Izzy stood there looking pretty, even in the rain and staring at Rob (she can do the wet hair look really well while I look like what Grandma would call a "drowned rat"). All the while I had my bum in the air, legs kicking around and my body halfway through the window trying to take out the CD, then unlock the door because Mum had locked them, for no reason!!?? So when I stood up I had a completely red face, and a MASSIVE line of oily dirt across the front of my top from Mum's filthy car - not a sight you want your 2 year ongoing crush to see.

Best day out turned into the worst!!

PS: I really don't know why Izzy is still bothering with Rob... he just totally airs her all the time.

March 30th - Good Friday

Neville had to go into work today because of some emergency and "a b***ard lorry driver who hadn't gone where he was told to go." Mum and I decided to have a relaxing day watching Netflix and eating junk food. We had a sofa picnic with loads of yummy stuff and watched Mamma Mia (again) and My Best Friend's Wedding. Mum likes things with happy endings - we are a bit the same. We usually cry at the same bits and always want everything to work out.

Mum has a new fad which is these cards with stuff written on. She had a whole bunch arrive from Amazon a few days ago. I thought one box would have been more "minimalist" than 5 boxes but she said they bring her joy and add value so they are allowed into the house on all counts. There are Law of Attraction cards, Angel messages, Moonology cards, Chakra ones and ones about The Universe. You are supposed to think of a question or ask a question out loud and then pull out a card that you are drawn towards. This card apparently provides the guidance you need.

Mum was showing me how it works when Neville arrived home and said, "What's this load of crap now then, Jaz?"

She said, "It's not crap - look I will show you by asking a question."
She closed her eyes, looked all serious for a few minutes and then
held her hands over the cards for absolutely ages (something to do
with "feeling their energy") until she finally pulled one of them out.
It said, "You are fully and completely supported by The Universe."
She nodded and smiled and said, "Oh yes, it's all making sense."

Neville said, "What is? What the hell does that mean? We don't
even know what the question was." Mum told him that isn't the
point because only she needs to know what it is she is seeking
guidance on.

Neville said, "Alright then. Here's a question .. 'Should I go to the
pub to get away from you, you total lunatic?'" Then he pulled a card
out and said, "Oh look it says, 'The pub will satisfy all of your needs
and desires.'"

Mum said, "No it bloody well doesn't Neville - stop taking the piss."

Mum went to restock the crisps and dips for us and I decided to
quickly ask some of the Moonology cards if I stood a chance with
Jake Lakson or if he even knew who I was yet. I pulled out a card
that said, "Take time to breathe out."

Seriously?? What does that even mean? I breathe out all the time.
What rubbish. Grandpa would call all this "a load of bloody
nonsense" and he's got a point.

1st April

Mum and Neville haven't talked about the famous shed for ages - which is fine with me, as it always ends up in a big row. Neville left Mum a really nice card in the kitchen this morning with a 5-pack of Curly Wurlys.

The card said:

I'm sorry about all the shed arguments, I think you are right, you deserve a special space you can use for your meditation area. We will sort something out. Love Neville Xx

She was dancing about in the kitchen looking really excited - I went off to see Em for a few hours because she's going on holiday in the morning. When I got home Mum was in a really bad mood. Turns out the card was Neville trying to be funny for April Fools Day! He isn't sorting the shed out and he hasn't decided it can be for Mum.

So annoying! And such a good example of why Neville is NOT funny.

2nd April

Mum is not speaking to Neville - even though he keeps saying, "Come on Jaz, it was just a bit of fun." She said her need for a personal meditation space is "no laughing matter."

It's Easter Monday today but we haven't really done much - it's been rainy with freezing wind so we have kind of hibernated apart from me seeing Em for a bit. Neville did shampoo the carpets at one point because he has a new carpet shampooer and is really pleased with it. Like a new toy. Bit sad if you ask me. Maybe he SHOULD get a shed to put boring household stuff in!

In fairness the carpets looked really nice and everywhere smelt lovely after he did it. Unfortunately about 2 hours later I heard him shouting "You little shit" from upstairs. The idiot dog had decided to go and do a great big wee on the newly cleaned carpet. She hasn't wee'd indoors since she was really little. I bet she only did it to annoy Neville - he did refuse to give her a sausage when he made his sandwich earlier, so maybe he had it coming.

I hope the weather warms up for next week because we are going away somewhere for a surprise. The dog is really fed up as no one has wanted to leave the house for the last few days because of the weather and she really, really wants a walk. Poor thing. I don't usually feel sorry for her because she is a total git most of the time (weeing on the carpet is good example), but she looks a bit sad right now.

4th April

Em face timed me from Portugal. She is staying in this villa that belongs to a family friend - it has a heated swimming pool and really pretty gardens. It looks soooo nice and it's MASSIVE! I don't even know where we are going for our surprise. I know it's not abroad, but I hope it's not rubbish. At least Mum's chosen it, not Neville, he's no good at that stuff.

The Applebys are in Florida at Disney - Mum says she has literally never seen so many photos from one person's holiday. EVER. I'm not sure that's true - she posted about a MILLION herself when she went to Bali. I know Mum says it's all a commercial rip off but it looks really fun.

The twins mostly look like they are having a good time - they seem to have met every single one of the Disney characters and been to a million different restaurants. Mum spoke to her friend Jennifer (she knows the Applebys really well) and she said it's not all as "perfect" as it looks. Apparently the twins have been arguing every single day and there have been lots and LOTS of tears (none of which feature on the Appleby Adventures page). She is bribing and threatening them before every single photo to make sure they look really happy and like they are having fun. Mrs Appleby told Jennifer it's mostly that they all have jet lag and no one is really sleeping very well. However, Jennifer told Mum that Mr Appleby told her husband they are having a terrible time. He is angry because the priority passes don't seem to be making the queues any quicker, he's bored senseless and Mrs Appleby gives in to every single tiny demand from the twins and never says no to anything. He's also annoyed that she chose Orlando when he wanted to go surfing in Hawaii because she says #familycomesfirst.

Every single one of the photos say #thehappiestplaceonearth #makingmemories #magic #dreamscometrue

#bestfamilyvacationever but Mr and Mrs Appleby are actually grimacing a bit in most of them.

Mum has spent pretty much all evening chuckling to herself and saying things like, "So, it's not all happiness in paradise after all." I think it's a bit mean of her to be pleased that they are not having a good time, but they are actually REALLY irritating.

It's a shame they feel like they have to pretend everything is perfect all the time just for social media. Mind you I can't talk ... I just posted a smiley picture of me and the idiot dog on Insta and put #besteasterholidayever. That's not true. It's been TOTAL SHIT!

8th April

We have just got back from a weekend away "glamping" in a thing called a pod. Mum booked it as a surprise treat at the end of the Easter holidays so that we could all "get back to nature and bond as a family" - I thought that sounded really lame but actually it was brilliant fun. We were staying in this little wooden hut thing in the middle of some woods and we had our own little area with a table and fire pit and thing to put a BBQ on. It was really peaceful and had a little stream running down the back and all the spring flowers were starting to come out in the woods.

There was a small double bed and a little kitchen and a toilet and I had a futon sofa that pulled out and turned into a bed. It was really cute and cosy but the WiFi was absolutely rubbish!! I was really, really fed up about that, but they thought it was great because it was like the "good old days" when families actually talked to one another and played board games. Mum kept on about it being important to take time away from technology and appreciate the simple things in life. Luckily I managed to get a one-bar phone signal by standing on the edge of the wood, getting Neville to lift me in the air and holding my phone as high as possible, so I texted Em and got her to do all my streaks for me - phew !!!

Mum and Neville were so annoying!!! Mum kept on about spiritual awakenings and humans being designed to be out in nature. She said she wanted to use the time to really appreciate the silence and totally relax and recharge her batteries. She kept saying how wonderful it was to hear the sound of the rain on the roof and wake up to the birdsong at dawn. Neville said he supposed that was true, except there was some sort of racket off and on. He said, "That'll be those sh*tting peacocks Ruby you mark my words." I don't know what he's on about, I haven't seen any peacocks.

So while Mum was all about the peacefulness, Neville kept going on about the trip reminding him of when he was in the boy scouts as a kid. He kept acting all manly because he lit the fire pit and cooked us some bacon outdoors. Mum said he should stop showing off about making fires, since using charcoal and fire lighters and a bag of logs from Tescos hardly made him Bear Grylls!! Neville got a bit sulky after Mum made the Bear Grylls dig because he'd been feeling so pleased with himself. So he had too many cans of beer and ended up tripping over a tree root and falling in the little stream. Luckily the shower was really nice and hot, because Mum said he wasn't allowed back inside our pod until he'd sorted himself out and stopped smelling like a stinking pond.

It was quite sad to leave at the end of the weekend - when we were packing the car Mum said that she passed a weird kid outside one of the other huts. He had strange long hair and just stared at her in a really sinister unblinking way for ages. She said it gave her the creeps and that he'd probably grow up to be a serial killer. She comes out with some weird stuff! But I was actually quite glad we weren't staying another night after that. She said something to Neville about how she should never have read "We need to talk about Kevin" - whatever THAT is.

When I told Grandpa about our weekend he shook his head and said, "What do you mean you took duvets with you?? That's not camping … what a load of bloody nonsense. I suppose you even took the kitchen sink." I don't know why he said that, I'd already told him there was a little mini kitchen in the pod. To be fair Grandpa was a cub scout leader for years so he does know a thing or two about camping. I spent ages trying to explain to him that it was "glamping" not "camping" but he said there's no such thing and that people just make up words "willy nilly" nowadays.

I like the expression "willy nilly", I also like "palava" and "gobbledegook". Neville said, "I like the word discombobulated, because that's what I feel like most days living with your mother."

April 11th

Arrhghghghhhhh, I have sooooo much homework to do. I hate how the teachers give you loads of homework the first few days back after the holidays. So unfair!!

Went downstairs to get a snack. Mum was in the kitchen messing around with a green juice in a mason jar, trying to take a really cool shot of it to put on Instagram. She kept moving it to a different part of the worktop and putting piles of spinach next to it. She only does it to pretend she is being really healthy ... and because Jasmine has been posting these amazing pictures of food and healthy smoothies on her Insta page. She's just trying to compete. It's pathetic. She did one the other day - she spent hours creating this masterpiece with bits of celery and ginger around it, posted it on Instagram with a bunch of hashtags about nourishment and health and then ate a big bag of Maltesers straight afterwards. She got a few likes though which cheered her up.

The worst part is she has actually started calling Instagram "The Gram" - it's UNBELIEVABLY ANNOYING - I can literally feel my myself getting angrier when she says it.

Honestly - this is an ACTUAL conversation that happened today in our house!!

Mum was busy googling pictures of holidays - she always does this as soon as we get back from a holiday. She is always saying you should live in the present moment and not worry about the future and then spends half her time planning and dreaming of some time waaaay in the future. I don't get it!!

Anyway she found a bunch of pictures of places that she would love to see and kept saying, "That would look good on the gram!" So here's how the conversation went:

- Mum: That would look good on the gram!

- Me: Don't say that - it annoys me

- Mum: Why?

- Me: It just does - it's annoying!!!!

- Mum: Everything annoys you!! Anyway I enjoy annoying you (she starts laughing)

- Me: Yeah but it really annoys me when you annoy me

- Neville: (chimes in) Well it annoys me when you are annoyed that she (points at Mum) is annoying you

- Mum: (laughing) It annoys me when Neville finds it annoying that you are annoyed by me annoying you

- Me: (very pissed off) It annoys me that you both think this is funny

The two of them were just laughing hysterically by now, so I walked out of the room.

That is quite possibly the most annoying conversation I have EVER had with the two of them.

The next time I came downstairs Mum and Neville were kissing in the kitchen. Yuk!! Revolting. Still, makes a change from them shouting at each other. Maybe they won't get divorced.

April 13th

Mum's having a right rant about Jasmine's Insta page. Turns out, she hired this amazing team of a stylist, photographer and chef to create a massive library of incredible photos for her to use on all her blog posts. I told Mum I thought the pictures all looked really good. She just snapped at me, "Well of course they do, they will have cost enough, but it's totally misleading, she's making it look like this is the kind of thing she just throws together every day for lunch and dinner. What NORMAL mother has time to do that kind of thing? Talk about making working mothers feel inadequate! "

Neville suggested to Mum that she set up a page with "alternative" food posts from "real mothers" with stuff like crisp sandwiches on a bit of kitchen roll, smiley potato faces or a bowl of Weetabix for dinner. I thought that would be quite funny but Mum seems to lose her sense of humour when it comes to Jasmine.

Mum managed to regain her sense of humour when she saw that Debbie had made a big jug full of one of Jasmine's green smoothie drinks for her kids and it had made them all sick. She is currently busy cleaning up bright green vomit from various bits of the house.

April 14th

I got up really late and Mum and Neville were sitting in the kitchen eating bacon and egg bagels and giggling at Neville's iPad.

When I asked what was so funny he said, "That tosser Appleby seems to be going for Dad of the Year." Turns out that Mrs Appleby has gone away on a hen weekend and Mr Appleby is entertaining the twins.

Neville said, "Blimey - it's a packed bloody schedule. Bowling, Frankie and Benny's and the cinema last night. So far today they've been to Go Ape this morning and they are currently "building their own pizza" for lunch. You don't "build" a f**king pizza FFS, what's wrong with these people? You buy it from a bloody shop !!!"

Mum said, "Shut up Neville, what's that photo there?"

Neville said, "Looks like tickets to an indoor skydiving place and a climbing wall. I expect they'll fit that in between having a nutritious 5-course dinner and Terence sodding Appleby managing to split the atom."

I told Neville not to be so mean. He's probably just jealous anyway - he never thinks of cool stuff for us to do. He won't be Dad of the Year in a hurry!

He said, "I'm not being mean Ruby. I thoroughly enjoy their posts. To tell you the truth, one of the only reasons I go on Facebook is to see what those smug gits have been up to. Their trip to Disney a couple of weeks back was possibly the highpoint of my entire year."

April 15th

Maisie had a party yesterday - we saw some pictures on Instagram. Dan told Izzy that Megan took something with her from her Dad's alcohol cabinet (she didn't know what - she forgot the name of it - but it was clear and she put it in her school water bottle). Her and Maisie drank loads of it and they were both really, really sick. Maisie got to the toilet in time, but Megan was sick all over the carpet outside the bathroom door. Dan said it was totally disgusting.

April 16th

EVERYONE is talking about the vomiting thing at the Maisie's party. Both "The Ms" look really bad today - like really pale and ill looking.

Mum is reading a book called "The Judgement Detox". It's all about not judging other people or yourself.

I was telling Neville all about "The Ms" and she looked up from her book and said, "I can't believe they are drinking at their age. It's terrible. What did Maisie's parents say?" I told Mum they weren't even there - they'd gone to the pub for the night. So she said, "Oh my God, that's totally irresponsible. In that case they deserve to be scrubbing vomit out of the carpet."

Neville said, "Stay away from those girls Ruby. They sound like trouble, you mark my words."

Like I would EVER be friends with them.

April 23rd

There is another royal baby. It's a boy, but it doesn't have a name yet. They have lots of possible names as the Royals use the same names over and over again. There are even people taking bets - Albert and Louis are the most popular. Neville keeps sniggering about the name Albert. I don't know why, it's a perfectly nice name. Even Mum said they really shouldn't call him that.

April 24th

Neville announced that Ed Sheeran has currently sold 6 million copies of his latest album, which is "not bad for a scruffy ginger bloke."

I told him he shouldn't be so rude and he should actually listen to some of the lyrics because they are really good. Neville said he has actually listened to the album but he can't cope with the song about the supermarket flowers as it reminds him of when his Mum died.

I felt a bit bad after that.

April 27th

The new prince is called Louis. Apparently a "Prince Albert" is a giblet piercing - urgghgh - how disgusting. Someone was talking about it at school. Put me off my lunch. Still it explains why Neville was being so stupid about the name.

May 1st

Coco has been banned from watching Peppa Pig after she started pointing at various men in the street and saying, "You have a very, very fat belly just like Daddy Pig." Auntie Sophie said she has also started to be mean to Felix a bit like Peppa is to her brother George. Felix actually doesn't seem to mind too much and just laughs at her, unlike George on the programme who just cries all the time. But still, Auntie Sophie has come to the conclusion that Peppa just isn't a very good role model for a young child. Even though she isn't real. And she's a pig!

It led to quite a funny WhatsApp chat with Grandpa saying, "I think the world's gone mad if a child can't watch a silly cartoon without it causing some sort of psychological damage," and Neville saying "I think it's a real shame that Daddy Pig has to be portrayed as a useless, lazy, fat git. Hardly representative of modern fatherhood. Kids will grow up thinking all dads are fat and useless."

Neville was lying on the settee with his belly hanging out whilst he typed his comment so I just typed, "Yeah imagine that!" into WhatsApp and went off to my room.

Then Shanequa typed, "I don't know about role models yeah, but I never understood how they could drive to their house yeah? Like it's on the top of that massive hill and like the car doesn't fall off? It's like a VERTICAL hill - how does that work? "

May 2nd

Mum put on the family WhatApp that she'd been onto MumsNet to see if the Peppa Pig concerns were common or if Auntie Sophie was worrying about nothing.

Mum said, "So it turns out there are quite a few threads on this subject over the last few years, it was actually quite entertaining". She said the most common thoughts on the show in general were:

1) It's not unfair for Daddy Pig to be seen as fat and useless. He is in fact fat. He is also useless.

2) Miss Rabbit does a ridiculous number of jobs in the village, so she should surely look way more knackered than she does and people are concerned if she is paying the correct taxes.

3) Susie Sheep is a bit of a bitch - but then Peppa is a spoilt little git - so they deserve each other.

4) Why would Daddy Pig invite a family of wolves to live next door?

Grandma wrote, "They are pigs - pigs aren't usually thin are they? It seems quite a lot of fuss about nothing and at least they are learning a bit of alliteration at a young age."

Uncle John appeared on WhatsApp briefly writing "Hahaha. Nice one Coco, it's perfectly fine to go round telling fat people they are fat. Someone should."

Then Auntie Eleanor appeared and wrote, "Don't be ridiculous John. Fat shaming is enough of an issue amongst teens and adults, the fact that 2 and 3 year olds are now blatantly fat shaming passersby, is a seriously worrying trend."

Then Neville piped up, "Just don't get me started on Postman Pat, I've got some pretty strong opinions on the so-called work ethic of that f**king twat."

May 7th

It's a bank holiday so I have the day off school. Neville had to go to work to cover for someone, so he was a bit fed up. Mum went off to lunch with a friend. It was another really nice sunny day so I hung out by the river all day with Alice, Em and some of the boys.

Debbie's kids all have the "Summer Flu" according to Facebook. Mum said she's pretty sure there is no such thing, but they are all ill with sore throats and high temperatures. There was a photo of the oldest girl with really greasy hair, looking all clammy and red in the face bundled up on the settee. I wonder if she knows that photo has been put on Facebook? I'd be furious if Mum did that to me!

May 9th

Apparently Debbie's youngest kid took "Barry" the class bear home today.

I remember we used to do that in school, in different classes with different toys. You had to do stuff with it for a few days, and fill in the diary talking about all its adventures and take lots of photos. Mum always hated when I brought one home and said it just encouraged competitiveness amongst the parents. I remember sometimes the toys got to do really cool stuff with other people like go swimming and to the cinema, or the Zoo. One year Eric the class Elephant actually got to go to St Lucia with Oscar's family for two weeks!! But whenever I had it we forgot to take it anywhere so had to make a bunch of stuff up on a Sunday night. Or Neville took stupid photos of stuff like the toy passed out surrounded by beer cans, or driving the car, or fighting with another toy.

I'm guessing Debbie's kid hasn't recovered from whatever the weird summer flu illness was .... she's just thrown up all over the class bear. Mum says it's going in the washing machine, but I wouldn't want to be the next kid to have it - urghghhgh!

May 10th

So there is officially a heat wave in England. You'd think people would be happy as we've had the longest winter EVER and it's been raining for like 4 whole months and been freezing cold. But people aren't happy, everyone is moaning that it's too hot. There are old men walking round town with hardly any clothes on and lots of sunburnt people. Harriet's dad was walking around in just a pair of shorts - we saw him outside Costa - he has a great big belly that hangs over his waist - that was all sunburnt too - it was disgusting -

urghghgh !! Everywhere you look people are mowing their lawns - it seems to be the first thing grown-ups do when the sun comes out. That and go to the pub.

It was horrible at school in the heat. We had to wear our tights and blazers which was awful. And PE outdoors was horrible. Lilly and Amelia's team made things worse by cheating and ruining the game for everyone. Miss Willis said it was just a game and not to worry about it. Mum said it's ridiculous, she said the teachers are obviously too soft and cheating shouldn't be tolerated. Mum said in her day all the PE staff were nasty sadists and they were sent out in all weathers to do hockey and cross country with bare legs and no jackets.

Neville is moaning about the fact that everyone is sharing photos of the dials in their cars that show how hot it is. He just keeps saying "It's f**king boiling, we know it's f**king boiling, I don't need to look at hundreds of pictures of temperature gauges to know it's f**king boiling."

He did this when it was freezing too. He's SO annoying.

May 15th

It's still really hot - the heatwave is carrying on. The good thing is we've had a BBQ for dinner every night for the last 4 nights. Mum said we need to make the most of it in case this is actually our whole summer and we don't get any more good weather. Neville is happy because he gets to put things on the BBQ and stand around looking important - it's a couple of burgers - anyone would think he was on MasterChef.

It's done nothing but rain this year but Neville keeps saying, "One week of sun and there will be a hosepipe ban - you mark my words".

We are having a Royal Wedding party at the weekend - there will be loads of us so it's a good job it's going to be sunny! Also Neville gets to ponce about on the BBQ EVEN MORE! BBQs are always the same. The men stand round the BBQ looking really smug and the women prepare all the food and run around clearing up and Neville or whichever other bloke flipped a couple of burgers takes all the credit for the whole thing.

May 16th

Debbie's kids are all vomiting again. She thinks they had a dodgy batch of burgers, as they were a funny colour and smelt a bit weird when she got them out of the freezer. Why would you cook meat that smells weird??

May 19th

Prince Harry and Megan Markle are getting married today.

Neville is already in a bad mood and stomping around the house muttering. He hates the royal family - I don't know why, they don't do any harm. Mum is all excited about the party and keeps saying, "I love a royal wedding" and going on about the time she camped on Pall Mall overnight to see Princess Diana when she got married.

Neville will cheer up once the blokes arrive and he can have some beer.

I better go and help Mum get sorted as people will be here soon - I can't help for long though, I told Mum I need AGES to do my make-up. I should have made some other excuse as this just sent her off on one of her usual moans about how I don't need make-up and I look lovely without it. She said, "It's a beautiful sunny day why don't you get some sun to your face instead." By the time I went down to be helpful, Neville was already drinking beer and getting a sunburnt head and I couldn't see Mum anywhere. I said to Neville, "Where's Mum, she said I should come and help?" He said, "I dunno - putting some slap on I expect" and got himself another beer.

The party is finished and Mum and Neville are trying to clear up. They are both hammered, so I think they should just leave it until tomorrow. It was a really fun party - everyone had royal family masks on which looked a bit freaky but made for some great photos. It was really hot all day too.

Me and Mum watched snippets of the wedding before people arrived. Megan is so beautiful!!! She looked amazing and not even like she had make-up on. There was an American preacher who I thought was quite funny - all the royal family sat there looking a bit awkward - I think it's because they are very reserved and he was being very enthusiastic. It did go on for a bit but he said some nice things. Kate looked very tired but very lovely. Mum pointed out that she only had a baby a few weeks ago so is bound to be tired. Neville said, "Rubbish - it's not like she even looks after the baby, they have a nanny for all that. She's probably stressed because Prince George and Princess Charlotte are little shits and she doesn't know what they might do at any moment."

I didn't get to see all of it so Mum said we can watch the BBC highlights tomorrow. That will probably be better because you don't have to sit through the boring bits.

Just as I was getting changed for bed there was a load of banging and smashing from downstairs - I thought I'd better check if they are both OK. Mum was sleeping soundly through all the noise ... she was crashed out on the sofa wearing a Camilla mask and hanging onto a glass of wine for dear life and Neville had fallen over the glass recycling box and knocked empty beer and wine bottles all over the patio. I took the glass out of Mum's hand and put it in the kitchen and suggested Neville leave it all for now, but he said everything was totally under control before smashing his head on the back door.

I left him to it - last I saw he was stumbling about swearing and rubbing his head with one hand, while the dog was following his every move, because he still had a left over burger clutched in his other hand.

May 23rd

I'm trying to watch old Friends episodes but the sound is being drowned out by Mum and Neville having a massive row about the credit card bill. According to Neville there is a 'load of expensive girlie shit' on there. Mum has bought a whole load of natural chemical free toiletries, skin creams, shampoo and deodorants. I just heard Neville shout EIGHTEEN POUNDS for a small shower gel Jaz????? EIGHTEEN F**KING POUNDS??? You can get Radox for a quid in Asda ... what were you thinking?"

Mum said, "Well, Jasmine recommended this company on the blog so I thought they must be good." So Neville said, "Oh so all of a sudden you are following that woman's advice, that's a bit of a turnaround isn't it?"

She said they are all "cruelty-free and vegan as well" and went on to explain all about the nasty toxins and parabens causing diseases like cancer and how we should be "as careful about what we put ON our bodies, as we are about what we put IN them."

Neville replied, "Oh and I suppose there aren't any toxins in Pinot Grigio then??? The number of bottles you lot rinsed through at Bridget's last Thursday would have easily supplied a small Italian wedding."

May 26th

Mum has started to do something called "The Miracle Morning", this involves her getting up at about 5.30am and doing a bunch of stuff like meditation and journalling and visualising. It's supposed to be making her more productive. Seems to me it's making her have more afternoon naps!! The worse bit of this is that it's made her obsessed with something called affirmations. These are statements starting "I AM" which are supposed to make you strong and confident because apparently if you say them often enough you start to believe them. Sometimes she stands there saying them into the mirror - she looks like a NUTTER!!!!

Last night was the worst - it said in her book something about a guy that used to shout his affirmations in the shower and it made them really, really powerful. I was trying to do my homework when I heard a bunch of shouting. At first I thought it was Mum and Neville having another row but then I realised if it was a row, it was a really weird one!! Mum was yelling stuff from the bathroom like:

I am powerful

I am successful

I am strong

I am confident

blah blah BLAH!!

I was just about to yell out "I am trying to get a bit of peace" but Neville must have felt just the same, because he suddenly shouted really angrily from downstairs "and I AM .... going to the f**king pub to talk to normal people." Then he slammed the door so hard the dog came scurrying upstairs and hid under the bed.

May 27th

It's half term and I'm really bored because as usual EVERYONE is on holiday apart from us. Mum keeps saying we are going to Croatia in the summer and Iceland in the autumn which is more than lots of kids get to do and that I should be grateful. Neville keeps saying, "You should count yourself lucky Ruby, when I was a kid the best we got was an afternoon at Skegness, you lot are spoilt rotten."

I asked Mum to take me to Grandma's house for a couple of days - at least I can just chill there without people moaning at me!

May 29th

Shanequa's staying here for a few days too. Uncle David and Auntie Sally are at a wedding in Scotland. Shanequa didn't want to go. She said, "D'ya know what Grandma? Even though it's like part of this country, Scotland is like a REALLY long way in the car?"

Earlier on Shanequa put Jeremy Kyle on but Grandpa turned it off again because he was listening to Radio 4. He said, "You shouldn't be watching that sort of mindless rubbish Ella, you should be reading a book and learning something useful."

Shanequa said, "I do learn stuff Grandpa, like stuff about DNA and genetics and all that. There was this bloke yeah? And he thought that this kid wasn't his kid, 'cos it was ginger, so they did a test. So like, it turned out, that he WAS the Dad yeah? So like even though him and the mother was dark haired, it was still his kid! It's a really good programme." Grandpa went off muttering something about wasted education. As soon as he left the room, Shanequa put it on again and then Grandma came in and turned it off because she wanted to listen to The Archers.

Shanequa said that Danny was coming round in a bit, so she needed to get ready.

Later on me and Grandma were having a cup of tea and trying to find out what Shanequa and Danny were going to do.

- G: So are you off on a nice date then?

- S: Dunno really, there's a party later? Might go.

- G: A party? On a Tuesday? Odd night for a party, will there be many people there?

- S: Dunno - might be dead, might be lit?

- G: Lit? Lit? What does that mean?

- Me: It means like exciting Grandma, really good.

- G: Oh, so my episode of The Archers is lit is it?

- S: OMG. No Grandma. It isn't. Ruby tell her will you? Hang on Danny's here.

Shanequa let Danny in and gave me and Grandma a hug goodbye.

Grandma said, "It's a bit early for a party isn't it?" and Shanequa replied, "Nah we're not going to the party yet Grandma. Going for a cheeky Nandos. Gassed."

Danny grinned and said, "Yeah Bruh, I RATE Nandos" and Shanequa said, "Give it up Fam, you rate everything."

The next morning Shanequa looked really, really tired. Turned out it was a very late night. She was sitting at the table resting her head on her folded arms, while Grandma was asking her all about the party.

- G: So how was the party then?

- S: I thought it would be like really rubbish but it was soooooo good. Like amazing. Seriously. Wig snatched.

- G: Who had a wig?

- S: You Wot?

- G: You said there was a wig. Who's was it?

- S: It's not an actual wig Grandma. OMG. Look I've gotta go. I'm like well stressed. I've got like bare college work.

- G: Bare? Who's bare? The person who lost the wig?

- S: OMG seriously. I can't even. Tell her will you Ruby?

May 31st

We ended up going to see some old friends of Mums (called Cathie and Richard) for a couple of days, on the spur of the moment kind of thing. We walked the dogs and played lots of fun games, so actually it was quite a nice break in the end. They had a massive games box with stuff like Jenga, Pie face, Tumbling Monkeys and loads of old school games and we played Scattergories which got the adults arguing about the words they picked but was quite funny. I actually didn't spend much time on my phone which was really weird.

Cathie has a crazy terrier called Derek - which BTW I think is a BRILLIANT name for a dog. I like human names for dogs. He is a bit mad though - he is scared of the sliding door in the patio and barks at it ALL the time and he can jump really high in the air especially if he sees an animal on TV. Our Idiot doesn't seem to recognise anything on the TV. Anyway, the Idiot spent the whole two days chasing Derek around the house and trying to furiously hump him. Poor Derek - he looked quite relieved when we left. Mum's friend Suzie got the Idiot a Fit Bark last Christmas so we can monitor her steps each day. Turns out she did 23k (in like actual distance, NOT in steps) in 2 days!!! That's a lot. So considering the actual walks we went on were quite short, that must have pretty much been the chasing and humping.

She slept for 2 solid days when we got home - she was totally exhausted.

June 3rd

We went to a wedding this weekend. It was in this amazing huge old stately home type place - with a lake and a little church in the grounds. Really posh. It was actually friends of Auntie Sophie's getting married, but Mum designed all the wedding invitations, and RSVPs and sign boards and table placements and stuff so they invited us along which was really kind. The signs everywhere looked really good and the flowers were beautiful! I met a few kids about my age but mostly I looked after Coco - there was a separate place for the kids to play and eat so they didn't disturb the speeches and stuff at dinner time. Auntie Sophie left Felix with Uncle Marc's parents who don't live very far away - good thing really he'd have been a right pain!

All the adults drank loads, because all the alcohol was free and so most people were in a right state - apart from Mum and Auntie Sophie, who were both driving. Neville, Marc and one of Marc's friends spent ages with their arms round each other's shoulders talking complete rubbish and waving beer glasses around. Whenever I walked past I heard stuff like, "NO. Seriously mate, you are SUCH a good bloke. No I mean it, I really do. You are a TOTAL legend." Honestly. Idiots.

A bit later a very old song called Living on a Prayer came on and loads of them were singing along (well screaming along) really loudly to it and one of Auntie Sophie's friends was in the process of stripping his clothes off on the dance floor. I suddenly realised that Auntie Sophie was looking a bit upset and telling Uncle Marc off. It turned out that Uncle Marc and his mate had just been found on the roof by a security guard. They were trying to steal a Union Jack flag off the top of the building.

Auntie Sophie was soooo worried because they were really drunk and it's a really high building, so it was actually really, really dangerous. She was telling him he needs to stop behaving like an idiot now that he has children and be more responsible.

Uncle Marc looked genuinely sorry and a little bit tearful and was obviously apologising and saying he wouldn't do anything like that ever again. So Auntie Sophie turned back to talk to Mum. As soon as she did Uncle Marc stomped over to Neville and said, "Well, APPARENTLY I'm not allowed to play on the roof."

Neville burst out laughing and spat a massive mouthful of beer all over one of the bridesmaids. Poor girl.

June 4th

Mum said over dinner that Auntie Ellie is really upset about the state of the world. They had a long chat today apparently and Auntie Ellie was in tears. Yesterday a boat sank near Tunisia and 48 migrants that were escaping from Syria drowned, and the same day in Thailand they found a dead whale with like 80 bits of plastic in its stomach. Also President Trump and the people that work for him are separating immigrant children from their parents in these big camps. It's horrible … all those poor little children, they must be so scared. No wonder Auntie Ellie is upset.

People are all very different really. Neville always says, "Just don't worry about it Ruby." Mum says that she tries to stay away from bad news because it brings negative energy into your life but that it's also important to show compassion for others as well (not very helpful). But Auntie Ellie says you need to feel all the difficult emotions and the pain because it will force you to fight for change. She says if people like Nelson Mandela and Martin Luther King hadn't fought for things that mattered to them then the world would be a different place.

I sort of know what she means but some of this stuff is so horrible it's hard to think about it.

June 7th

I found a really good quote on Instagram today that was so relatable. Mum called it a meme…. it's not a meme, it's a quote !! That's so annoying.

Anyway it said:

You think I'm listening but I'm really doing your brows in my head

Then Mum posted one on her feed. I am pretty sure she did it just to annoy me - it said:

I'm old skool. I actually wake up with my eyebrows already on my face

She thought it was hilarious and was delighted because she got so many likes and laughing/crying emojis from people HER age. It's not funny. And she called it a meme again.. urgghghghhghahghh!

June 8th

I am still annoyed about the eyebrow thing from yesterday - Mum keeps chuckling about it - what does she know anyway? She grew up in the 80s - they had terrible eyebrows, really bushy - almost like mono-brows!!!!!!

And they had terrible hair. Grandma has a "wall of shame" and there are some hilarious pictures of Mum with her mad hair. She actually had a mullet!!! Seriously!! And all her friends had these crazy perms including the men!! There are photos online of these really ancient bands and all the men look like poodles!

June 9th

A load more migrants from somewhere drowned near Yemen a couple of days ago. I saw this on Auntie Ellie's Instagram - her account it is literally ALL about horrible stuff. I'm going to unfollow her I think, it's making me really sad. All my other accounts are fun stuff and make-up. I don't really need to know about war and death and stuff.

June 11th

Mum and me just had a row, so I'm in my room - I'll leave her to cool down for a bit then go and give her a cuddle and say I'm sorry - that usually works. She threatens all sorts - like taking my phone and iPad away usually, or no more sleepovers, but as soon as I give her hugs and kisses and get a bit tearful she gives in. Grandma says I have Mum "wrapped around my little finger" and "kids get away with murder these days". I like all Grandma's expressions. The best one is "you don't know you're born" … what does that even mean? Everyone knows that they were born!!

The row was about me wanting a new bikini - everyone is going to be hanging out down by the river this weekend as this heatwave is carrying on and my old one doesn't fit. I found a really nice one online at New Look but Mum said even if we ordered it now it wouldn't be here for tomorrow because that isn't enough time. Then she said we need to be careful about buying stuff all the time, because we are becoming minimalists and buying stuff is just supporting a society that is more and more obsessed with building up material possessions … and she said "money doesn't grow on trees." Honestly! I know that - what a stupid comment. Even the Prime Minister said "there isn't a magic money tree" and she must know since she sort of runs England.

Honestly!!!! It was only £9.99 in the sale as well. It's not exactly a fortune. She doesn't mind spending that much on a bottle of Prosecco! Presumably drinking loads is totally minimalist!

June 12th

When I got home from school the kitchen was a complete disaster - pans everywhere and dirty baking trays and food processor full of gunk. Mum said she was making healthy energy balls and sugar-free oat cookies.

Neville got in from work and starting moaning about the mess. He went to get a beer from the fridge and said, "What are those things that look like little round shits?" Mum got angry and said, "Don't be disgusting Neville, those are the energy balls, they are really tasty." He wanted to know why they were "shit-coloured" and Mum said, "They aren't, they are just brown from the dates and the raw cacao powder." He still insisted they looked like the little poos that Felix did in the bath the other day that bobbed around on the top of the water. Auntie Sophie had to fish them out and disinfect the bath!

He wasn't impressed with the oat biscuits either. Mum said, "You make them with bananas and apple sauce so they are still sweet but with no refined sugar." Neville said, "But it's horrible, it's all soggy. There's no crunch. Give me a hobnob any day of the week."

Mum said she is trying to find healthy alternatives to sugar and said, "Don't you realise Neville, sugar is completely addictive. It's has EXACTLY the same effect on the brain as cocaine or heroin. It's literally a modern day drug, that's why people find it so hard to give up."

She also said, "Once you've detoxed your system from processed sugars you'll find the natural sugar in things like dates and honey and fruit is sweet enough. It's much better for you and you don't miss all that manufactured sweet rubbish anymore."

Neville replied, "Well how come I saw you eating a bag of skittles earlier?" It looked like the start of another one of their pointless arguments so I stuck in my headphones and went upstairs.

June 16th

Mum received a magazine called "Nature" in the post - I thought it was because she is always banging on about how important it is to spend time in nature. Turned out Auntie Ellie had sent it. There was a massive post-it note on an article about Antarctica, which is apparently melting at an accelerating rate. It said it's melting by 200 billion tonnes a year which will be 3 trillion tonnes in 25 years.

I'm not very good at maths and amounts of stuff but that sounds like a LOT of melted ice.

Neville said, "Well if you think that's interesting Ruby, look at this. There's a raccoon in Minnesota that climbed to the top of a 23 story office block! He's an internet sensation."

Neville must just google obscure stuff - he finds the weirdest news stories.

June 18th

Oh god - here we go - Mum and Neville are having a screaming row downstairs. They are doing that so much lately (even though Mum keeps going on about how she has been experiencing so much more inner peace since she started The Miracle Morning). I had to put my headphones in to drown them out. They usually argue about whatever Mum's latest fad is.

Oh no - I think I heard the word shed. I'm seriously going to ring Grandma and find out how much a shed is and if they can just help me buy one !!!!

I just heard Mum tell Neville that he's a "total imbecile" and that "he just doesn't understand her need to be connected to her highest self."

Then I heard him yelling, "What highest self Janice? You're only 5 foot 1"

June 20th

There is a really weird smell in the house. Mum is wandering around with a sort of bunched up bit of paper that she's set light to, wafting it around and pointing it at the walls around the house. It never surprises me when she is doing weird stuff, but I like to know what is going on and WHY she is doing it.

She said, "I'm doing a "full clearing" of the house with a sage smudge stick to realign the toxic energies and make the flow work more harmoniously." Well Duh! Why didn't I guess that! She said she has to walk clockwise round the house making sure each area is cleared. Honestly I have no idea where she gets some of her stupid ideas from.

Neville came in and said, "Blimey Jaz have you been smoking weed?" She said, "Don't be ridiculous Neville, it's a sage smudge stick." He said, "Well, it smells like weed to me." Mum said, "Neville don't say stuff like that in front of Ruby." Honestly do they think I don't know anything.

Then he added, "Canada made recreational marijuana legal yesterday - you never know, England might not be too far behind."

June 24th

I've been upstairs for ages in my room. When I came down Mum and Neville were in the garden drinking wine and chatting. Neville was looking at his phone. He said, "Look at this Jaz , your sister has put 'what a momentous and exciting day' on her Instagram." I'm guessing he means Ellie, because Auntie Sophie doesn't have time for Instagram between doing her important job and looking after Felix and Coco.

Mum leant forward and said, "Ooooh that's exciting perhaps she's met someone. Wouldn't that be lovely." Neville said, "Yes Jaz it would, but no it's not about that. Do you know what this excitement is about ? Do you ? Apparently, as of today a ban has been lifted and women in Saudi Arabia are now allowed to drive for the first time. Christ her life must be dull if that gets her all fired up."

Mum said, "Shut up Neville - you know she is all about championing women's rights and if this is something that has really made her day, then that's nice isn't it?"

Neville said, "She needs to have a few glasses of wine and chill out a bit if you ask me."

Wine is Neville's answer to everything. No wonder he left school without any decent exam grades.

June 29th

Mum is in London on a day out. They are supposed to be shopping and having lunch. So far her Instagram is entirely photos of glasses of wine and cocktails. There's the Champagne bar at St Pancras Station, there's a gin bar, there's somewhere with lots of flavoured vodka. Mum has salted caramel ! There is not much food or shopping going on by the look of it. There were a bunch of embarrassing photos of them posing with one of those statues in Convent Garden that don't touch the ground and are actually people staying really, really still. The man did really well to carry on acting while they were all being really stupid around him. Just before I went to bed there was a video of them in rickshaws being taken back to the station. They were all shrieking with laughter and yelling things at people they passed on the street. Then Bridget fell out the side of the rickshaw. Instead of helping her get up Mum carried on filming it. OMG I feel so sorry for the poor guys that are riding the rickshaws - worst nightmare customers EVER !

June 30th

Felix is one today!! We all went into London because he was having a little party in a church hall. Mum was still looking dreadful from her day/night out yesterday and spent the whole journey there slumped in the front seat of the car with her sunglasses on barely saying a word.

We found the place easily because Auntie Sophie gave us pretty good instructions and there were tons and tons of balloons lining the walkway into the hall. Mum perked up a bit when we got there because even though it was a party for a 1 year old Auntie Sophie and Uncle Marc had invited lots of their friends and so they'd put on a really full bar to keep the adults happy whilst this bloke called "Mr Music" entertained the kids. Most of the kids ran round banging into the walls if they were old enough to walk or just sat there staring at Mr Music, looking a bit gormless. A few of them just cried. Some of them perked up a bit when he did a few songs that Neville called "crowd pleasers". Songs like "hop little bunny hop hop hop" and the one when all the cows are asleep and the Dingly Dangly Scarecrow starts singing. There was a bit of giggling and some wiggling around to those. I joined in a bit and danced with some of the older toddlers like Coco because it was really cute. Mostly though, the mums and dads were more enthusiastic than the kids.

Neville kept making comments about Mr Music, saying that it wasn't right for a grown man to be doing a job like this and that there must be something wrong with him. Mum told Neville to shut up and Uncle Marc said he'd just given Mr Music two hundred quid, which wasn't bad to just put on a dodgy outfit and sing a couple of songs for an hour.

Neville said, "Fair comment mate, perhaps I'm in the wrong job."

When they got to the cutting the cake bit, Auntie Sophie was trying to take photos of Felix and all the other guests and wasn't in charge. Felix was supposed to blow his candles out but he didn't really understand. Uncle Marc gave him the great big cake knife to hold and he was waving it around in the air really dangerously. Luckily Uncle Dave spotted it before Auntie Sophie did and got it out of Felix's hand.

Neville and Uncle Dave spent the rest of the day saying, "You were only supposed to blow the bloody candles out" in these stupid voices. They thought it was really funny but I didn't get it.

July 2nd

The heatwave is full on - we have fans in the house and don't have to wear blazers to school or tights which is pretty cool - although I have to make sure I remember to do my legs.

Mum is in a really happy mood since it's been so hot but Neville is moaning a lot more. He says it's because he keeps forgetting sun cream and burning his bald head. He looks weird actually as he has one of those tans where he looks like he still has a white t-shirt on. He was mowing the lawn with his top off - like ALL the old people are doing - and honestly, he looks like someone has boiled his head bright red. Even Mum said he should try and even out his tan. He said he was too busy working for a living to swan about in the sun.

Unlike Mum - she went into town to take some stuff to the post office and bumped into Helen and Bridget so they went to the wine bar for "one" glass of wine. They've put a load of comfy outdoor sofas there where you can sit in the sun and watch the world go by - one turned into quite a lot more AS USUAL !! She was supposed to get me from hockey practice but I ended up having to walk back and sit there on my phone while they carried on drinking and cackling. At least Bridget's daughter Evie turned up - she's in the year above me but we get on really well. Her eyebrows are PERFECT ! So we had a really good time and even made fun of them all a few times (which they totally didn't get because they were too hammered by then - typical !). They FINALLY decided that they should go home and sort out dinner for their families and all wobbled off in different directions.   Honestly! Pathetic.

Mum said she couldn't be bothered to cook so I ended up with a frozen dinner from the Sainbury's local instead.

Actually it was pretty cool because it reminded me of being a little kid - she got me chicken nuggets, smiley potato faces and a packet of penguin biscuits. She tried to cut me some slices of cucumber mumbling on about me needing my 5-a-day but I thought she'd slice off one of her fingers so I took over and did it myself !

She muttered something like, "Did you like it ? It's kind of a retro dinner ! I should have got you some Alphabetti Spaghetti to go with it" and then passed out on the sofa.

July 4th

Everyone in the UK is happy at the moment because of the heatwave and the football. England are in the world cup and it's making people very excited. It doesn't mean much to me as I don't really know much about Football but according to Mum, England are crap and never get very far - she says the whole country gets really worked up and thinks they will do well and that this is their year but they never do and then everyone is disappointed. Apparently the last time they won a world cup was the year Uncle John was born and he's really old. This time though apparently they have a decent team and they are doing really well. Even Neville is vaguely interested and he usually says he'd rather stick pins in his eyes or watch Downton Abbey (in that order) than watch any sport. Mum keeps saying it will only be a matter of time until they bugger it up as usual, but it's nice to see a bit of positive national spirit going on - especially with all the bad feeling over Brexit. Mum and Neville go on about Brexit all the time. I don't like to ask too many questions in case they talk about it even more.

I don't mind about the football actually - we have had a few really great afternoons and evenings in the sunshine at people's houses watching the football - Katie has a big screen in her summer house that you can see from her garden and so all us kids got to stay up late on a school night a couple of times and watch the matches, while the adults all drank loads.

There is also a football song on the radio all the time called "It's coming home" Neville gets really annoyed about it - saying things like "if it really does come home I'm a monkey's uncle !! " It's all about the lions on the kit from what I can work out and just repeats the words "it's coming home" a lot. Not very inventive lyrics as far as I can see.

A few people suggested meeting at the pub late afternoon today as it's glorious weather again. It was only supposed to be an hour but it turned into about 4 hours so Mum and Neville are in a bit of a state. They bought me a load of chips at the pub, but it's not exactly dinner is it? I had to make myself a cream cheese bagel when we got in.

They were going to FaceTime Uncle John and the family to say Happy 4th of July, but they weren't in a fit state, so they ended up sending him a text and crashing out in bed early.

July 7th

England have beaten Sweden 2-0. There are flags sticking out of people's cars and everyone is going on and on about it coming home. Football and sunshine seem to be pretty good at making adults happy.

The politicians aren't very happy though - they all keep resigning.

July 9th

Neville said Boris has now resigned as the Foreign Secretary the day after the Brexit Secretary resigned. He said he never liked Boris but now "that twat Jeremy Hunt" has taken over, whoever he is. I don't know who any of these people are apart from Boris - I remember him from the Olympics when I was younger - he seemed quite funny but now everyone seems to hate him. Apparently Jeremy Hunt is the person that ruined the NHS. None of the people that wanted Brexit seem to be staying in their jobs. Neville says that David Cameron, who was the old Prime Minister, thought it was a good idea to have a vote about Brexit, but ran off to a villa in Italy as soon as the results came in. Neville says he's ok now though, because he spends lots of time in fabulous houses in Cornwall by the sea. I thought Neville was pleased for him at first but then realised he was using his sarcastic voice.

Mum says that none of the Tories care about ordinary people and are only interested in No. 1. She said, "Never mind the rest of us

struggling, they will all be fine when the Brexit shit hits the fan" …
whatever that means.

Everyone complains about Theresa May all the time so I asked
Neville whether she is the worst Prime Minister EVER or if that was
David Cameron. He said "Hmm, it's a tough one Ruby. Cameron did
something revolting to a pig at school and once mislaid one of his
kids down the pub, and the worst thing The Maybot ever did was run
through a field of wheat, so normally I would say Cameron wins the
title. But right now she's doing a pretty good job of shafting our
Economy and the UK might eventually break apart so on that basis I
guess it's her."

I still don't get politics. Grandma is always saying that I should
listen to the Radio so I know a bit more about what's going on in the
world. Shanequa said, "Yeah Grandma, but it's not something young
people are worrying about." Grandpa got annoyed and said, "Well
you SHOULD be worrying about it Ella. Decisions being made now
will have a massive impact on your future." Then he went into this
whole thing with her.

- G: Well for instance Ella - do you know who the leader of
  the Labour Party is ?

- S: The wot ?

- G: The Labour Party

- S: Dunno .. is it that one with mad hair ? Boris ?

- G: (looking annoyed) No, it's not Boris. What about the
  Prime Minister - do you know who that is ?

- S: Yeah, I sort of know this one. I know that like Donald Trump is the Prime Minister of America. Do you mean like the English one ?

- G: Yes Ella the English one. And Donald Trump is the PRESIDENT of America, they don't have a Prime Minister.

- S: The English one… well that must Boris.

- G: Hmm He wishes !

- S: Wishes wot ?

- G: Never mind (shakes head)

July 11th

So England lost to Croatia tonight and now everyone is miserable about it. Neville just says that he could've predicted it wasn't coming home and should have made a bet down at the bookies whatever that means. The worst thing is he started to sing, "It's staying there, it's staying there .. football's staying there, it's staying there …. " loads of times. He thought it was really funny. We tried to tell him it's not funny at all , but that didn't work.

July 12th

Neville has turned his stupid idea of "It's staying there" into a full song for Chemical Banana to sing.

President Trump has turned up for a visit. Lots of people are protesting and they have a massive balloon flying over London that looks like a fat baby Trump in a nappy. It's very funny.

The fact he is here means that Mum is getting ranty and using a load of big complicated words that I had to look up on google - like cretinous, misogynist, egotistical and narcissistic. Neville used lots of words too but they were mostly twat and bellend so I didn't have to look them up.

July 13th

Chemical Banana had a gig last night for the first time since England lost in the World Cup three days ago - people that like football are still feeling a bit miserable about it but Neville decided to sing "It's staying there" in the pub anyway. Apparently there were loads of people lobbing sausage rolls at him and Josh Martin's dad called him a Co*kwomble"... He seemed quite proud of that. Josh is in my class - seeing him on Monday is going to be a nightmare !!

We are actually going to Croatia on holiday in a couple of weeks - it's a good job none of us like football so we won't care if they go on about the fact that they beat us.

July 15th

Neville said that Croatia and France played today in the World Cup and France won. Most people in England stopped caring about the tournament as soon as England lost and are just back to enjoying the sunshine and spending hours outside drinking a lot of beer and wine. We had another BBQ today - I never thought I would say this but I'm getting a bit fed up of burgers and sausages and salad.

July 22nd

YAASSSSS! We are going to the cinema to see Mamma Mia 2 - I LOVED the first one - I watched it over and over when I was little and Mum took me to the stage show in London which was BRILLIANT ! I was really small and had to sit on loads of coats to see the stage.

It must be the first time I've actually seen something when it FIRST came out at the Cinema - Mum usually makes me wait for the DVD to come out. I think we only went because she loved the first one too and ABBA was like a thing when she was growing up.

July 25th

So nice to be off for summer at last and hanging out with people. Mum and Neville are still working until we go away. I've been put in charge of walking the idiot dog most mornings to give Mum a break. It's a bit of a pain, but then I DID want the dog in the first place. It was actually my idea.

Me Izzy and Em have been hanging out all day. Izzy is going out with Dan - AGAIN ! She never learns. I bet there will be a drama within a week. They actually sat together in Costa today - like away from me and Em - as if they were on a real date. TBH it looked like a rubbish date. They were both on their phones and they didn't really talk. But Izzy took a selfie of them with their Frostinos and put it on Instagram. It said #costadate #couplegoals - honestly !

Frostinos are totally my favourite thing. There is a new one for summer - Salted Caramel Crunch. It's THE BEST.

Mum came home with pizzas for our tea and told us she'd just bumped into Jane who'd just been really told off by a scary woman at bible club for turning up late. I thought religious people were supposed to be forgiving. Mum said Jane's smallest daughter is going to bible club every day this week , not because they are religious, but because it's very cheap childcare. Apparently she is now walking around talking about Jesus all the time and singing songs and sprinkling confetti all over the house. She's trying to make the whole family pray. Jane is not impressed.

Izzy's family are Catholics and they go to church but most of my friends aren't religious and our family aren't either. Neville is always making jokes about "God-botherers." I once bought Mum a solar-powered wobbly-headed plastic Jesus figure from a service station when we went on a school trip. She still has it and says it's one of the best things I ever got her.

July 27th

We are all packing and Mum is running around yelling about the washing. We aren't even allowed to take much stuff because we are taking rucksacks. She told me not to pack a full make-up kit as it will weigh too much in the bag. So annoying. She said the cheap airlines charge you extra if your case is above the weight. One of her friends once took loads of clothes out of her case, when she was going somewhere on RyanAir, and put all of them on. She said she wasn't paying a penny more. I thought it was funny - she must have looked like Joey on Friends when he wears all of Chandler's clothes. They couldn't do much about it, so they had to let her do it, but she said she was really, really uncomfortable and hot on the flight!

I'm totally flying first class when I'm older.

July 28th

I've dyed the bottom of my hair bright pink for the holidays. We aren't allowed to do it in school. Don't know why, it's such a stupid rule! I LOVE it so much. Neville told me it looked really pretty which annoyed Mum because he NEVER notices when she has her hair done.

July 30th

We had to get up really, really early to go to the airport but I got a toastie from Pret à Manger in the airport and Pringles on the flight. We got to Croatia quite quickly and this really nice man from the Airbnb picked us up from the airport. He smiled loads and left us some fruit and bread and beers in the flat. The flat is up like a BILLION stairs but has a really cool view over Dubrovnik town.

Neville was really excited to come here because apparently it has something to do with a programme called Game of Thrones - I asked Mum if I'd like it but she said it's full of people dying in a really gruesome way and all the different families and countries in it are very confusing. And there are dragons. I don't like stuff that isn't realistic. Or stuff where people die horribly. Apart from Horrible Histories but that was quite funny.

We found the local supermarket. Everyone here is really friendly apart from the lady on the till at the supermarket, she kind of angrily throws our food in the bag. I think they are naturally friendly because it's always sunny, but I'm sure they are pleased that they almost won the World Cup.

Mum is moaning that they don't seem to sell any tonic but they do sell gin - she is having to drink gin and this kind of fizzy lemon stuff and is not very happy about it. Neville keeps telling her it's a #firstworldproblem. That's annoying.

Jane's family have got to their holiday villa - her daughter is making everyone pray every time they see an aeroplane, because that's what they told her at bible club . The villa is near an airport which is making it a bit of a problem. There are also 5 cats and a massive dog at the villa that weren't mentioned on the information. They are allergic to cats! Jane's daughter brought about 10 cuddly dogs with her so now there are 10 cuddly dogs, 1 real dog, 5 imaginary dogs that go everywhere with her daughter and lots of massive, massive poos all over the lawn. She says it's better than last year though when she accidentally booked them on a holiday to a nudist camp.

August 2nd

We have been in Dubrovnik a few days now and done loads of stuff. I wish we'd do more fun stuff at home but Mum and Neville are always too busy. We went on a cable car, we walked around loads and loads, we had amazing pizza, we've eaten like a TON of ice-cream, we went to a cool bar built into the walls of the city where you could jump off the rocks into the water and where Neville said you had to take out a small mortgage to buy a couple of beers and a Sprite. We went on a boat trip to this island with amazing turquoise coloured water and did some snorkelling. I'm doing loads of swimming - the water is really, really clear.

Here are some facts from the last couple of days.

26 = the number of flights of steps from the beach to our apartment.

40 = the temperature when we are walking up all the steps.

1,000,000 = the number of steps I reckon I've walked up in 3 days.

0 = the number of times we did the trip around the city walls today. It was too hot and really expensive. Mum thought it was going to be free so she said, "I'm not suffering in that heat, battling for space with a bunch of cruise ship tourists AND paying an arm and a leg for the privilege!"

There really are a ton of stairs and LOADS of walking but it's a lot of fun and the WiFi is really good. My Insta feed is full of brilliant photos with turquoise water.

August 3rd

Today we went kayaking around the walls of the town and around an island. It was pretty cool - we watched the sunset on the way back. The kayaks were for 2, so me and Mum went in one together and Neville got put with a random. She was called Deborah and was bit old. She told Neville that she was very good at kayaking but hadn't done it for a while.

He said afterwards, "I would put a million pounds on the fact that woman has never picked up an oar, never mind been kayaking." They were all over the place as Deborah had no clue and was constantly rowing in the opposite direction to Neville and their oars kept smashing against each other. Me and Mum were a good team as I've done kayaking on school trips tooutdoor activity places. We had our oars synched really well so we did great. Part way round there was a nudist section of the island - there were lots of naked men, jumping off cliffs with their giblets on display - yuk!!! Mum got some cool shots of the sunset on her iPhone.

After the kayaking we went to get some dinner at a restaurant overlooking the harbour. I was checking the comments on my Insta photos and Mum was on WhatsApp posting a picture of us in the kayaks at sunset for the gang. She said, "Listen to this Neville. Jane's family are at one of those waterparks with those massive inflatable things and every single time Jane jumps off one of them her boobs escape out of her swimming costume. She's trying to stuff them back in, in mid-air, the kids are absolutely mortified."

Apparently Helen's family are at Luton Airport getting ready to leave. Helen said there are like 50 million people there, she's had 3 rows with her husband, her youngest kid is in a right strop and won't eat any of the food anywhere in the airport and her teenager doesn't want to go on holiday anymore because the whole family annoy him. I know how he feels. Bridget's family are in Spain eating sea snails - yuk! Mind you, I think I'd rather eat sea snails than see men jumping off cliffs showing their giblets!

August 11th

We have moved islands and we are in our 3rd Airbnb. We are sort of backpacking, although Mum said if we were doing it properly we'd wouldn't have any accommodation booked and we'd just turn up to dodgy hostels hoping to find a bed. That or we'd be spending a fair bit of time sleeping on the floor in bus stations. I prefer the Airbnb option but maybe I will do it properly when I get older. I think it's only really backpacking because we have rucksacks instead of wheelie suitcases and we are using public transport. But to be fair we are spending a HUGE amount of time getting on and off boats and buses and lugging around our rucksacks, which is pretty much what it's all about according to Mum.

Neville said, "It seems to me backpacking involves just about getting settled into somewhere when you have to up and leave again, and packing and unpacking the f**king rucksacks every five minutes. Give me an all-inclusive hotel holiday, where I don't even have to MOVE from the bar, any day of the week." Mum said, "We'll go all-inclusive over my dead body. If it was up to you, it'd be all "Brits abroad", never seeing a single landmark and surviving on a full English every day. I can't think of anything I'd hate more."

I quite like a fry up so I'm not sure what makes that a bad holiday, but Mum obviously feels quite strongly about it because she added, "Frankly Neville, if that's your attitude, Ruby and I will go away without you next time."

Seems a bit harsh, but it might be quite nice without him for a few days.

The flat we are in at the moment is owned by a very old man. He lives in a flat downstairs so we keep seeing him all the time. He's really weird - every time we see him he holds my face in his hands, smiles and says weird stuff in Croatian. He told Mum he thinks that MAYBE his sons are a little bit old for me. Turns out his sons are 39 and 41 !! A BIT old ?? A bit. Neville keeps muttering, "How much for the leetle girl?" in a funny voice whenever he is nearby. It's creepy. I told him to shut up.

We are self catering so we don't "spend a fortune eating out every day" to quote Mum. It's actually quite hard because there is no oven, no sharp knives, no potato peeler, no other useful cooking utensils, no grill and no toaster. We do however have lots of bottle openers, tea lights and a very nice cake slice. Neville said, "If we fancy a romantic meal of beer and cake by candlelight we are sorted."

I've had lots of pasta with butter and sweetcorn. Mum attempted Greek salad, but despite the fact it's on every single menu in Croatia, we couldn't find any Feta in the supermarket - so she invented "Swiss salad" made with some dodgy sliced Emmenthal and served with what Neville now calls "G&FLs" (fizzy lemon).

191

Mum and Neville have now discovered a supermarket where you can buy a litre of white wine with a metal beer cap that costs about 2 quid. They like to sit on the balcony drinking it and watching the sunset. We have a window to the balcony that is also a door. It's a windor. Mum and Neville keep smacking into it after couple of large glasses of their 2 quid wine.

Oh and we are all having really weird nightmares/dreams, it's 40 degrees every single day and the light to the outside stairwell of the flat is located inside the apartment. It's NO USE when we get home in the dark.

August 13th

We went on a buggy safari in these little funny little mini cars with pedals and a bike engine. It was really fun and I had the Go Pro on a stick so I could take tons of footage. The only problem was the buggy me and Neville were in caught ON FIRE! We had to jump out and we were left behind in these woods for a bit. Mum was texting us from this beach wondering where we'd got to. The guys rescued us and gave us a new buggy. They didn't seem too worried about the catching on fire part and just said, "Is dirty fuel."

Neville told Mum that health and safety obviously doesn't mean much over here.

August 14th

We got on a ferry that was really late leaving. I don't think the Croatians are bothered about time. It was supposed to go to two different islands but they decided they weren't going to stop at one of them. All the people that were going there to visit or stay were a bit annoyed. The Captain was standing by the ferry smoking a cigarette and this passenger asked him what was going on.

- Passenger : When's the next ferry?

- Captain : I don't know

- Passenger : How long am I supposed to wait ?

- Captain : I don't know

- Passenger: Well what on earth shall I do ?

- Captain: (with a shrug) Have a beer and a sandwich.

Neville said he thought "have a beer and a sandwich" was a pretty good answer to most of life's problems.

The ferry was a bit rough but at least it went to the Island we wanted to go to. It had a sign on the entrance that seemed to be saying that you HAD to wear speedos and swimming costumes but you absolutely couldn't bring a dog or a suitcase onboard. Weird because there were loads of suitcases but there were no dogs. And (thank goodness) NO speedos.

On Helen's holiday her youngest kid said it's the worst holiday he's ever been on. So far he's complained about: t he hire car; the seatbelt in the hire car; the space in the hire car; the hotel bed (uncomfortable); the pillows (uncomfortable); the hotel room (has an ant in it); the sun (too hot); the sea (too cold); the pool (acceptable temperature, but there's a wasp in it) and every single item on the menu.

Bridget's family are now somewhere that has goldfish on the menu and Jane has just eaten oil pie (whatever that is) because all the menus where she is staying are in Greek. Neville said, "Well since they are in Greece you'd expect that wouldn't you ? Didn't she go to Oxford ? You think she'd know stuff like that."

Mum said, "The kids have worked out what the Greek is for "spag bol" so they are all fine now."

Oh and the man looking after the pool at Jane's villa IS wearing Speedos. And he's about 80. Yuk!

August 16th

It's still really hot - like 40 degrees every day - we haven't seen one cloud since we got here. But I'm getting a nice tan. Mum's been on What's App and said that it's the last day of Bridget's holiday. All the kids were looking forward to a lazy day just swimming in the hotel pool, but it's shut because someone's done a massive poo in there!

Helen's family are staying at a hotel that looks nothing like the brochure and it's full of people from Liverpool and Manchester that have loads of tattoos and keep fighting. They hired some bikes to go for a day out and explore, but her teenager hit a rock on a rough path and damaged his giblets on his handlebars.

August 18th

This is the last few days of our holiday. We've been jet skiing which was amazing and hanging out at the beach a lot.

At our last flat you could only make a sandwich or boil an egg because the only things in the utensils drawer were 5 different bottle openers and a cake slice. We are now in a place with a really cool modern kitchen, an amazing oven and loads of pots and pans and stuff. But the utensils are still really random. We have a strange chopping board that is in pieces that don't link together and something that Mum says looks like one of the weapons from Game of Thrones. We also have the longest wooden spoon in the world (and the shortest) as well as a small cake fork (but no cake slice just when we could have used one).

It's also very random in an apartment for 4 people to only have one teaspoon, one wine glass and one coffee mug.

Neville said, "Perhaps we could all take turns .. or we could drink out of this vast array of saucepans …"

August 19th

We did our last fun activity day today. It was really cool - it's called canyoning and Mum says it's kind of like white water rafting except you don't have a raft. We had to all get done up in a lifejacket/wetsuit/bum-harness combo because even though it's boiling outside, the water will still be freezing .

Mum and Neville look utterly ridiculous in their wet suits. Mum said, "No-one - and I mean no-one - can look good in this sort of get up." I don't agree as the fit instructors looked pretty good to me.

So we went to this huge river, we had to hike down the canyon, slide down rapids, clamber through rocks, jump off things and float past waterfalls. It was very cool and soooooo much fun.

Mum was a bit rubbish, because even on the fast rapids where everyone else kind of slid off perfectly, she ended up going in a different direction and smacking into the rocks - every single time! Good job they gave us helmets. And she swallowed most of the river by the look of it. She said afterwards it felt like she'd done 4 hours of solid squats and that the skin on her fingertips had all come off.

Neville said, "Never mind Jaz, look on the bright side, if they can't take finger prints then you can commit all manner of crimes undetected."

We took the Go-Pro with us canyoning and Neville got some really funny footage of Mum on the rapids. It's hilarious. Mum didn't think so though, she snapped really angrily at Neville, "For Christ's sake delete all of that, I look like an un-coordinated, rubber-encased whale !"

August 21st

It's our last night and we have to get up at silly o'clock for our flight home. Mum doesn't want to leave and has told Neville he will need to "drag her screaming to the airport"

Neville seemed to manage better at the canyoning than Mum but neither of them have walked properly since we did it! Mum is finding stairs really difficult and wincing a lot, which is a bit unlucky since we are somewhere that has SO MANY stairs. They must both have useless muscles. Perhaps they should actually do some exercise sometimes?

We went to a posh seafood restaurant tonight as it was the last night. I ordered calamari but it didn't come in rings like at home - it had all the tentacle bits on as well that I don't really like. I decided I couldn't eat them because they actually looked like poor little headless blokes and I started to talk to them in a cockney accent and call them names like Ralph, Norman and Terry. It made the waiter laugh so much he gave me free ice-cream.

Mum said it reminded her of when I was little and we were eating mussels in a restaurant and I picked one up and said really loudly to it, "Don't be alarmed, but you are about to be eaten." Mum said it made the whole restaurant laugh.

August 22nd

We got in from the airport and went straight to see the family. They were all at Grandma's for Sunday lunch and it's on our way home from the airport. Shanequa is going to the Reading Festival in a couple of days, she is really excited but a bit nervous too. It's just given Neville an excuse to get nostalgic and go on about Glastonbury (again) when she mentions it.

Grandma just keeps going on about the loos. The more everyone mentions the portaloos the more grim they sound. Grandma said it will be "hell on earth" and that Shanequa should stay home - but Grandma won't go anywhere unless she has her own private en-suite bathroom. They can't be that bad or I am sure no one would ever go to festivals. Mum always shrugs during these sorts of conversations and says that until you've been in a fly-infested long drop toilet, in 100 degree heat, in Africa, you don't know what you are talking about.

August 24th

Grandma rang and asked me to "translate" a conversation she had with Shanequa on WhatsApp

- G: Hello Ella, how are you getting on - are you enjoying the festival

- S: Hi Grandma. Yeah totally. GOAT!

- G: What? Why are there goats?

- S: There aren't!? Wot r u on about?

- G: You said something about a goat?

- S: Nah not goat … GOAT - seriously it is though. YOLO!! CU soon.

So I had to explain that it's a way of saying it's amazing and there aren't any goats. Grandma just kept muttering, "Are they playing the music on a farm?"

August 26th

Shanequa got back from Reading this morning. It was the last day but she'd had enough and came home early missing the headline band. It was raining too much and she was wet and tired and hadn't managed to have more than a couple of washes with a wet wipe for 4 days. Yuk! Neville kept saying it was a total travesty to go to all that effort and NOT see The Kings of Leon. And she didn't get any sleep because it was so noisy and her and the girls had pitched their tent under one of the floodlights so it had an orange light on it permanently and felt like daylight the whole time. I asked her if the portaloos were really bad and she said they were OK the first day but after that there was sick everywhere and people had rubbed poo on the walls. She also said that when you are in them people think it's funny to rock them so it feels like they are going to tip over and you'll get covered in all the poo. Urgghghghgh! That's persuaded me - I'm definitely never EVER going to a festival. I might have a really big festival party for my birthday next year - but that's different as it will just be in the garden and we can use the proper toilets in the house. "Proper toilets"... I sound like Grandma!

She told us all about some of the boys that had a massive fight on the second day and smashed into her boyfriend's tent and flattened it and then fell on two more tents, including hers and Riva's, flattening them as well. She had to put her tent up again!

Neville asked if she'd taken the opportunity to pitch it somewhere that wasn't under a massive floodlight but she said, "Oh yeah ... that would've been like, totally brilliant, dunno why I didn't think of that?"

August 27th Bank holiday

So the heatwave seems to be officially over!! It's rained ALL bank holiday weekend - it's SO miserable. It just puts everyone in SUCH a bad mood. Mum says that people in England just moan whatever the weather - she says that's why Australians call us "whinging poms" - she didn't say what a POM is - but I'm guessing it's an insult. Anyway everyone has stopped moaning that it's too hot and now they are moaning that it's too cold. Everyone I know has the heating on APART from us - as usual! Neville keeps stomping about and complaining if anyone DARES to say it's cold. He just said "what a load of f**king b*llocks I am NOT putting the heating on in the middle of summer, you lot are just making a fuss about nothing". For once him and Grandpa agreed with one another. Grandpa said that he doesn't know what is wrong with people and since when was 12 degrees cold?? He said in his day people put on an extra jumper and didn't moan about it. He also said in his day people knew what hard work was and these days people are just "work-shy layabouts." Grandpa doesn't know what he's on about - if putting up with Neville going on about the heating every 5 minutes isn't hard work, then I don't know what is!!!!

I decided to just hang out in my room all day watching Netflix. I watched "To all the boys I've loved before" for the 5th time! I am COMPLETELY in love with Noah Centineo. Mum really likes Lara's dad in the film! He's called John Corbett and apparently she loved him in something called "Sex and the City" and something called "My Big Fat Greek Wedding."

She was looking at the cast list on Google and said, "Look Ruby it says here John Corbett is in the 'hot dad' stage of his career. He's always been gorgeous, Carrie Bradshaw made a bad decision as far as I'm concerned. And did you know I was watching "My Big Fat Greek Wedding" when I was in labour with you."

Honestly, I don't need to know stuff like that. TMI. And who on earth is Carrie Bradshaw?

August 29th

End of the summer . ..

I hate when it gets to the end of the summer holidays - I love all the long days by the river and hanging out in town. Everyone's got a great tan and doesn't want to go back to school again.

Luckily there are 2 parties this weekend and Evie's party is a sleepover - she has a really big loft area in her house so I think about 7 of us are all sleeping over on air beds and stuff. I've just been to the shop and got loads and loads of sweets. Need to remind Mum to get Evie a present. I know she will moan about me having a better social life than her …

August 31st

It's still really hot. Auntie Sophie filled the little paddling pool in the garden for Felix and Coco to play - she sent us a really cute video of the two of them playing in there naked and splashing around. She said about 5 minutes after the video Felix did an absolutely massive runny poo in the pool and Uncle Marc had to scoop it all out with some rubber gloves on and disinfect the whole thing. Coco was really upset because she was having so much fun.

1st party was at this brilliant outdoor waterpark nearby - It's sooooo fun. Loads of big inflatables. It was perfect weather for it too.

Luckily because we aren't babies there were no pooing incidents. But I reckon a few people had a sneaky wee. It was James 1's party - I never know what to buy for boys so Mum just bought him 2 cans of Lynx and some Moams.

September 2nd

Brilliant sleepover at Evies ! Izzy spent quite a lot of time trying to talk about Dan and Rob and who she should pick - like there is a choice - Rob is soooooo not interested. We basically ignored her and talked about other stuff every time she mentioned either of them.

September 5th

Back to school. I'm in year 9 now. My new form teacher is called Miss Wilson and she looks really scared the whole time. She has a really quiet voice so most of us just ignore her in registration. There is a party , not this Saturday but next Saturday , at Dan's house. Megan and Maisie are planning to bring vodka. They are so sad but they think they are really cool. Maisie steals it from her parents and they don't even notice. I bet they are sick again !!

I told Mum and she said that I must always feel like I can tell her anything. Even if I think that she will be annoyed about it. Well I won't be telling her about vodka that's for sure - I won't be touching the stuff. Even Neville said, "They drink vodka ? Blimey, that's a bit hardcore for 14 - even I didn't drink that at their age and I had some seriously rough mates."

I said Megan is still 13.

September 10th

Coco has started at a private pre-school. There was a photo of her on WhatsApp in this seriously cute little uniform and a hat !! Her two new best friends are called Horatio and Badger.

September 12th

Coco has already received a special star award for a drawing she did at school. Auntie Sophie put a photo of her holding her picture in the family WhatsApp. Everyone said it was lovely apart from Uncle John who said, "Very nice - how much is it selling for at Sotherby ' s?" and "Is she fluent in Mandarin yet and has she passed all her violin exams? That's what all the child geniuses do isn't it ?"

I played the violin when I was little for a bit. Mum said she was quite pleased when I wanted to give it up. She said it made her want to cry when I played .. and not in a cute way !

September 14th

Mum is really angry with Neville as usual. She sent him a text asking him to get her something on his way home and he thought he was being hilariously funny with his reply. He was still laughing about it when he got home and said, "Did your Mum show you?" I said she hadn't, so he showed me instead.

It said:

Jaz: Can you pick me up some antiseptic cream at the chemist ?

Nev: Yes, I have opposable thumbs

Jaz: Twat !

I don't know what opposable means. But I DO know he's very annoying. But I told him it was very funny, just so he'd shut up about it.

Coco is no longer friends with Badger. He called her a pleb , because she lives in a terrace house.

September 16th

It was Dan's party last night. Megan and Maisie put a picture of themselves drinking the vodka on Instagram before the party. They must have felt stupid or been worried someone's parents would see because they deleted it again. When they got to the party they just sat in the corner and wouldn't talk to anyone. They are so weird. At the end of the party Megan randomly kissed Dan, who she doesn't even LIKE, so Izzy left the party in tears. I think Megan did it on purpose. Em was coming home with me for a sleepover , so we FaceTimed later to check Izzy was OK. It was a bit of a drama, but she said she will get over it.

Neville made us pancakes for breakfast and Izzy did a FaceTime while we were eating them. She said Dan had messaged her last night. She said that Dan said he wished that Megan hadn't kissed him because it was totally disgusting. Izzy asked him if it was because he thinks Megan is ugly and she is prettier, but he said it was mostly because Megan had been eating cheese and onion crisps.

Neville said, "That's exactly how your mother feels when I've been down the pub and had a pickled egg."

OMG - Pickled eggs ?? Why is that even a thing ?! Helen always has them at her parties. GROSS !

September 18th

Less than a month until my Birthday - I'm not having a party this year so at least there won't be any drama !

I had to escape from the kitchen really fast earlier because Mum started to say, "Right Neville … about this shed …." So annoying. The shed talk is bad enough, but even more annoying I was about to get myself 2 Mr Kipling apple pies from the pantry. Now I have to STARVE.

September 19th

OMG so many tears today. Dan sat with Megan at lunchtime and then there was a photo of them at Costa after school. Izzy has been crying her eyes out for hours. Her face looks a right mess. Mum told me to tell her to lie down for half an hour with some cold bits of cucumber on her eyes, otherwise they will be all puffy in the morning.

September 20th

Turns out the Dan and Megan thing yesterday was a bet ! Dan's mate Alfie dared him to make it look like it was a date in exchange for a copy of Call of Duty Black Ops 4 (which is an 18 +). It's because Alfie and some of the other boys really hate " T he Ms" and wanted Megan to look really stupid ! Bit mean really - but it's only Megan.

Dan told Izzy that he wanted that game for ages and his parents wouldn't let him have it. He said he doesn't like Megan at all and he should have warned Izzy it was a bet so she didn't get upset. That seemed to work so now Izzy is smiling again and taking selfies with him. Megan and Maisie have been sitting on their own in the canteen looking really angry!

Neville said, "Which ones are Megan and Maisie again" and Mum said, "The two redheads that dress like hookers." I thought that was a bit harsh, but Mum made me show him a picture from the party of them all dressed up. Neville looked at the photo and said, "Blimey Jaz, I see what you mean. Bit rough."

Mum keeps saying if anyone in my year will end up pregnant whilst they are still at school it will be one of those two. I think for once she is probably right.

September 22nd

Mum keeps putting embarrassing rubbish on Instagram. Because she works from home she puts stupid stuff about working in her pjs and "the long journey along the corridor to her office" So SAD. Today she put this stupid thing about planning her work Christmas party which will just be her. It's sooooo not funny. All my friends think that because she works at home the house must be tidy and I must get real dinners and homemade cakes and stuff. THAT could not be further from the truth ! Neville often comes in and says, "Have we been burgled Jaz ? Look at the state of the place."

She always says that "everyone" lives in the house so "everyone" is responsible for keeping the place tidy. I completely agree - Neville totally needs to do more round the house. His shoes are all over the floor in the hallway - there was nowhere to dump my school bag or my coat.

I got myself a crumpet, but there weren't any clean mugs and I wanted a cup of tea. Mum got really annoyed and said, "Why don't you check in your room then, I don't dare go in there, there is so much crap all over the place." She talks SUCH rubbish. I went off to do my homework. It was a bit embarrassing actually because I found 4 dirty plates and 7 dirty tea mugs round the room. Oooooops. I sneaked them downstairs without her seeing so I didn't get nagged again !

September 26th

When I got home from dance tonight Mum was all tearful in the kitchen - she'd dropped the shepherd's pie that was for dinner on the floor and the plate had smashed into pieces. Her and Neville were trying to get the idiot dog out of the way so they could clear up all the broken bits of the dish, but she kept nose diving into the mince and trying to eat it all. I think she probably swallowed a few bits of china TBH.

Mum was really upset and kept on about being really clumsy all the time and muttering stuff about something called "the change." Neville kept telling her it was fine, she said, "But there's no dinner and look at the state of the floor." Neville said, "The furry Dyson will sort all that out." Then he went to the Chinese and got us a take away for dinner which was brilliant - MUCH better than shepherd's pie.

He also got Mum some gin which seemed to cheer her up!

September 28th

Some really weird stuff is going on in the world. In the news today it said that a seal slapped a man in the face with an octopus !!! It's mad. It was in New Zealand and the man was kayaking and this seal just came out of the water and walloped him with the octopus right in the face! Neville saw someone on twitter say something like "what must someone have done in a former life to make a seal twat them in the face with a Cephalopod." He just kept chuckling about it and using the word Cephalopod a lot. I had to look up it up on Wikipedia - I've never heard that on a David Attenborough documentary. Good job that didn't happen in Croatia when I was kayaking. Though to be honest I think if a seal was going to appear out of nowhere and wallop any of us it would have chosen Neville... it's the sort of ridiculous thing that WOULD happen to him.

October 3rd

We are getting up really early tomorrow to go to Iceland. I am
having a few days off of school because Mum told them I'm going
to learn a load of stuff about Geography. I don't even care about
Geography really but it seemed to keep school happy. I asked
Neville why we had to get up soooooo early EVERY time we go on
holiday and he said it's because Mum likes to get the really cheap
flights and they all leave about 5 in the morning. If Pret à Manger
isn't open that early I won't be very happy.

Izzy sent a Snapchat saying I wasn't really missing much at school,
but that Dan made a comment about Alice looking really pretty since
she got contact lenses so she dumped him again.

October 4th

We are staying in a seriously cute Airbnb place and I've got a
sofabed. The WiFi is so good (way better than at home) and we even
have Netflix on the TV - it's brilliant - just like not going away.
Mum didn't look impressed when I said that, she said the whole
point of travel is to "open your mind and appreciate other cultures."
She also wants me to learn stuff while we are here. Sounds pretty
boring to me.

We couldn't get into the Airbnb for a few hours after we arrived so
we went to a pub to keep warm. It is TOTALLY freezing. Mum and
Neville made one beer last about 2 hours as everything here is really,

really expensive. There was an old man in a corner who was either asleep or dead (not sure which) - his mouth was hanging right open. I videoed him for a bit as it was so funny and sent it to Em.

In the morning we have to get up early AGAIN and go and get a bus to go to the Blue Lagoon. Neville says the Blue Lagoon is a "must visit" place in Iceland and that it's like a big hot tub in the middle of nowhere.

October 5th

The Blue Lagoon was amazing !!! It's brilliant - I had a slushy drink and put a special silica mud mask on my face. It made my skin feel really good. We had our phones in little waterproof cases and got lots of fun pictures. Mum and Neville had a beer even though it was 9 o'clock in the morning. Neville said, "When in Rome." Obviously he's the one that needs to learn some Geography.

It was a great day. We put lots of pictures on the family WhatsApp and Auntie Sophie said that Coco thought it looked beautiful and just like the film Frozen. She also said people "shouldn't have beer in the sea", so now Neville calls her the "Fun Police."

We are spending the next two days on buses going all over the place looking at waterfalls, glaciers, black sand beaches and volcanos. We get picked up from bus stop 10 near our flat. That would be fine but guess what ?? Iceland has a PENIS museum ! Seriously !! and it's opposite the bus stop that we have to go to. I've had to look at it twice today and will have to look at it again tomorrow AND the next day. Unbelievable ! Who needs a museum about giblets ?

I think Mum and Neville did this on purpose. They claim that they didn't and they knew nothing about the museum. I'm so disgusted and they just think it's funny. There are actually t -shirts with giblets on, there are little furry TOY giblets ! And just inside the door there is a sculpture type thing where there are two big round stones and one really long stone. HONESTLY !

Mum and Neville just keep giggling about it and telling me I should have more of a sense of humour. It's NOT funny and they are both pathetic if you ask me.

October 8th

We are home now - we had 3 freezing days and lots of time waiting for buses and looking at the giblet museum. But I suppose we did see some pretty cool stuff. The ice shapes at the glacier were really cool and we also saw these things called geysers, that shoot boiling water out from way down inside the earth. That was cool and I videoed it to show Grandma. Mum was really annoying though, she kept insisting I took my headphones off and listened to the boring man on the bus telling us all about the country instead of listening to my music. I suppose some of it was quite interesting, like the stuff about them having hundreds of earthquakes every day but you mostly don't feel them.

I'm glad to be back. I actually missed the idiot dog a bit. She was so excited to see us, it looked like her tail was going to fall off. She also couldn't bark. She's obviously been making such a racket at the kennels the last few days, she's actually lost her voice !

October 10th

I will be 14 on Saturday. 14 - it's amazing ! I've got 7 girls for a sleepover in the lounge on Saturday and on Friday 3 of us are going out in town for pizza after school. I had a big party last year and I want a REALLY big one next year so Mum said this one has to just be a little "get together" not a big thing. I suppose that's fair but kind of wish I was doing something a bit fancier.

I told Neville if his present to me has ANYTHING at all to do with Chemical Banana I won't speak to him for a week !

October 12th

So my birthday celebrations went well ONCE I got home and after Em, Alice, and Evie arrived and went out to the Pizza place. School was rubbish though.

So on my last birthday Kaleigh and a bunch of others decided that they needed to announce they were Lesbians. And today Kaleigh decided she isn't a Lesbian anymore , or she might not be, she doesn't really know. She's not sure if she identifies as a girl or a boy. She is still Kaleigh for now, but she likes the name Kyle because she thinks she probably identifies more as a boy. Why does she need to use my birthday to make these big announcements ? Honestly, it's all anyone is talking about.

When I got home from school I was trying to explain to Neville that she isn't a Lesbian anymore but she's probably non-binary so we can't call her she or he we have to call her 'they'. Neville looked utterly bewildered and said, "What do you mean she doesn't know if she's a girl ? Of course she's a bloody girl."

Mum tried to tell him it's not that simple and explain the variations of transgender and gender neutral and non-binary in the whole LGBTQ community and said that, "He really ought to educate himself about the modern world." He just kept shaking his head and saying, "Is this another ridiculous millennial fad ? At the risk of sounding like your Dad it's a bit of a bloody nonsense."

Mum said, "Don't be so offensive Neville!" in an angry voice, and then I explained that Kayleigh said her, sorry "their", Mum had written to the school to make sure they were handling stuff like getting changed for PE and using the toilets in a sensitive way.

Mum was just saying, "Well I'm sure schools have policies and just tailor it according to the individual" when Neville interrupted and said, "So she - sorry "they" - are going to go in the boy's toilets and piss in the urinals are they?" So I said of course not, they could still go in the girls if they wanted or use the cubicle in the boy's toilets if they needed to. Then he said, "Not if someone was in there for ages doing a massive dump they couldn't."

Mum said, "Ignore him, he just doesn't understand diversity at the best of times." But I was just disgusted that FOR ONCE we were trying to talk about something serious, and he had to talk about pooing !! That's so typical.

Mind you, on that subject, Auntie Sophie put in the family WhatsApp that she had to do an emergency nappy change for Felix in the back of the car at Tescos, and he did a massive projectile poo that shot across the car park and only just missed a grumpy old man with a trolley.

October 14th

Brilliant sleepover. We made a hilarious video. Izzy apparently now HATES Rob having been IN LOVE with him for like EVER. Mum wanted to know why she hates him now and if he did anything. I said I didn't know - I didn't even ASK Izzy why. So much drama - who needs it? Although I totally doubt he did anything - he pretty much totally ghosts her.

She said she might go out with Dan again. Honestly - that's pretty annoying.

We faced timed Grandma and Grandpa and Auntie Sophie was staying there with Felix and Coco - we said hello and they were going off for their bath. Grandma was asking me all about the sleepover and I was just telling her about the presents people got me, when Coco appeared again completely naked and shouted, "Felix did a poo on the floor" into the iPad.

October 15th

They are banning phones in school at break and lunchtime !! Unbelievable ! We can use them if we absolutely have to in lessons but if we get caught using them at any other time they are being taken off of us and given to our parents! It's soooooooooooo annoying.

Mum and Neville think it's a good idea, that it's important to limit "screen time addiction" and it will mean we actually talk to each other at break and lunch which is more healthy. That's annoying - like we don't all talk to each other already. Even worse, they told me this whilst sitting on 2 separate sofas on their separate phones!

Just when I think they can't annoy me any more. If anyone has screen time addiction, it's the two of them.

The only good bit about the phones is that I won't have to look at a million selfies of Izzy and Dan every day. They are a thing again - I am so bored of it.

October 16th

We played UNO today at lunchtime with some of the boys and I found a game of finger twister online and printed it out - it was really funny. No one really missed their phones apart from Izzy who said it felt weird not taking selfies. In the end she went off to the toilets for ages to do her hair and pout into the mirror anyway.

October 17th

Izzy's had her phone confiscated. She is NOT happy. Miss Willis caught her messing about with it on her lap in the library and loading stuff onto Instagram. Talk about stupid. EVERYONE knows Izzy NEVER goes to work in the library out of choice. She is blaming Dan but she's the one that's always taking pictures not him. And he wasn't there anyway because he was playing UNO with the boys.

October 19th

It's the last day before half term and Megan has been making a total IDIOT of herself sending messages to Dan and trying to flirt with him. Izzy says she isn't bothered, because right now this is the longest her and Dan have been together without one of them dumping the other one. She says she's "completely secure in the relationship." Mum said that is good, and that it means they must have a clear idea of what the other person is thinking and feeling and "honest communication is really important to ensure harmony between couples."

Neville was sitting in the kitchen with a beer and snorted really loudly when Mum said that. Mum said, "What now Neville?" to him in an angry voice. He said, "Honest communication? That's a bloody laugh, you've completely refused to tell me what the f**k you've been sulking about since last Tuesday." And he added, "Don't bloody well take relationship advice from your mother Ruby." Then a row started up - as usual !

M: (Shouting) You know EXACTLY why I'm pissed off with you Neville

N: No I bloody well don't. Why do you think I keep saying "what's the matter Jaz" every five f**king minutes ??

M: Well if you don't know I'm not telling you.

N: That's my entire f**king point.. and you bang on about honest communication ?

M: Well if our core values were more in alignment, then I wouldn't need to explain every little thing now would I ? You'd be able to feel instinctively when I was disconnected at a deep soul level.

N: Well, what I feel instinctively at this moment in time is that you are a right f**king pain in the arse.

October 25th

We just came back from visiting Mum's friend Margaret. She lives a long way away in the Lake District - it's really pretty when you get there but it takes about 6 hours. I downloaded a whole bunch of films to watch on the iPad. Only problem was the car overheated and we had to sit in a service station for 2 hours waiting for the AA. Mum and Neville got annoyed with one another even though it wasn't anyone 's fault. At least we were by the shops, so there was a really good range of snacks and toilets nearby. Better than sitting on the side of the road.

The AA man was called Steve. He was really nice, but he decided to tell us absolutely everything he was doing. Neville was standing next to him staring into the engine , trying to pretend he knew what Steve was on about. In the meantime, Mum was keeping Margaret informed with constant updates. Margaret said she had plenty of wine chilling ready for when we got there.

Mum's messages said:

OMG Steve has not stopped talking.

It's like being in a mechanic's class. Neville is doing SUCH a good job of looking interested.

Seriously Steve …. stop f**king talking and get on with it. Honestly Mags, what I don't now know about the diagnostic testing of cooling systems is not worth knowing.

We are on our way now, except Steve is following us. Hopefully only to the next service station and not all the way to your house !!

OMG Steve is talking Neville through his entire report and doing a full debrief.

Seriously Steve's days are f**king numbered !!!!!

Steve finally fixed the car, and we carried on driving, for hours! When we finally got to Margaret's house, the adults stayed up late and I went off to snuggle in the room I was in and talk on Snapchat to some of my friends. They all looked terrible in the morning, but perked up a little bit after Neville made a big fry up. It was something to do with Limoncello . .. not sure what it is, but it obviously makes them very drunk. It was a really nice couple of days - we went to see where Beatrix Potter lived and wrote all her books. That was kind of cool - I used to love those stories when I was little.

October 27th

Debbie's kids are ill again. She is very unhappy, because it ruined all their plans for half term. Mum said they were supposed to drive to Scotland, but she couldn't face the journey with loads of sick buckets in the car. They all had a sick bug, but it kind of went in circles because as soon as the last one stopped being sick, the first one started up again. The people at the cottage in Scotland refused to refund the money when they phoned to cancel. Neville said, "Silly cow, of course they aren't going to refund them because the kids are all vomiting. What planet does she live on ? Seriously?"

Jane's family are up North somewhere visiting her father-in-law and his wife (she really doesn't like his wife - she's not her husband's mum and Jane calls her "the old harridan"). She doesn't approve of people drinking so there are no wine glasses in the house. There are two tiny sherry glasses. Jane said she's already had 12 glasses and still hasn't finished a bottle of wine. The first night they were there, she made them dinner because she was trying to be nice but his dad and Beryl (the wife) said they had terrible tummy upsets the next day and accused Jane of poisoning them with her cooking. She told Mum, "I obviously didn't poison them, because we are all fine, but to be honest I'm quite relieved they have the sh i ts as it means we can have a day out on our own."

Mum is all over the place laughing one minute and in tears the next - it's a bit like Izzy! Neville said it's definitely her hormones. She said she felt better because Bridget said she feels the same. Bridget wrote on WhatsApp "You'll be menopausal the same as me Jaz. I told my family yesterday that bursting into tears, laughing like a hyena then screaming like a demented witch - all in the space of 2 minutes - is perfectly normal."

October 29th

Izzy and Dan haven't broken up yet. It's amazing. Mind you Dan's been away in Tenerife for half term so they haven't actually seen each other. Neville said, "Sensible bloke. Giving women a bit of space is the only way to keep them happy Ruby, you mark my words."

Mum is always going on about "creating space to allow good things to come in." Perhaps Neville is finally listening to her. When I asked him if that's true he said, "Well..I don't exactly LISTEN to her Ruby, she talks quite a lot of shit most of the time. I pretend to listen - you know - I sort of nod along in the right places."

They seem reasonably happy with one another at the moment, so he must be doing something right.

November 1st

Halloween was actually REALLY cool yesterday. It's soooooo good having Halloween in half term ! We had the best party at Alice's house and went trick or treating beforehand. Izzy had a huge row with Dan the minute he got back from Tenerife. She spotted a girl in a few of his holiday photos. He said she's the daughter of the people he went on holiday with and the 2 families have been friends for years. She accused him of fancying her and spent half the party in tears.

She is SUCH a drama queen.

November 4th

It's firework time again. Mum is moaning (again) about all the noise complaints on Facebook. The dog (again) is not in the least bit bothered. Neville took a photo of her lying on her back completely asleep and posted it on Facebook saying "OMG the dog is totally traumatised." He thought it was funny.

Debbie put on Facebook yesterday that after all the drama last year, she wasn't taking any chances with the fireworks this year, and got a prescription for special calming medicine for the dog. The dog obviously wasn't too keen on whatever was in the medication, because Neville just shouted down the stairs, "Jaz? Have you seen Facebook? Debbie's dog has been shitting all over the kitchen for the last 2 hours ! Explosive diarrhoea it says here. Nice !!"

November 5th

It's almost 100 years since the First World War finished. We are doing loads of stuff about it in school. Grandpa put in the family WhatsApp tonight that we should all switch on the TV and watch the evening news. He said they are playing the last post and lighting all these torches in the moat at the Tower of London and it's very moving. We put in on and it looked really pretty. They are going to be doing it every night up to the 11th November to celebrate the Centenary.

Shanequa typed, "That looks sooooo cool, but I don't get why it's 100 years"

Grandpa put, "Oh for goodness sake ! The war finished in 1918 and now it's 2018, so that's 100 years"

Shanequa put, "Oh yeah, that makes sense !! You just know SO much stuff Grandpa"

He said, "Well Ella, you should know all this too, you did history at school didn't you ? They must have taught you about the First World War?"

So she said, "Well yeah … course . .. we did all that stuff. I'm not great with like, the EXACT dates, but I know all about Hitler."

A little message came up saying "Jack Brady has left the group" [That's Grandpa - he must have got REALLY fed up – he always rejoins again after a few days]

Uncle John appeared and typed, "I reckon Coco knows more about history than you do Ella. In fact, I think she's already passed her A levels and got a place at Oxford"

Grandma put, "Stop it John, leave her alone"

Even I know that Hitler was World War 2, so I wrote, "Shanequa, you need to watch Black Adder 4 - then you'll know all about World War 1"

And Neville wrote, "Yeah .... hahhaha ... to quote Baldrick, the war started because a bloke called Archie Duke shot an ostrich 'cos he was hungry."

So Shanequa put "Wot ? I can't even" and then another little message came up saying "Ella Brady has left the group."

November 8th

So the little kids are doing WW1 stuff at school as well. The Applebys are building a replica of a First World War trench. I remember doing stuff like that. There would be a big subject every term and you had to do something like make a model or do a painting or a video or something like that. I usually did a video because I LOVE making videos, but loads of the boys always made models. Well … their dads did !! There were always loads of amazing models that were totally not made by kids.

Mum has been watching the progress of the Applebys' one for about a week - it's insane!! It's like a work of art. Neville said it actually looks like the full set design for a Hollywood war movie!

November 9th

OMG. I thought dramas at school were boring. Adult dramas are sooooo much more boring !

Mum and Neville had an actual argument about the contents of the man drawer in the kitchen. For someone that is always going on about "keeping your vibration high" and "not focussing on things that drain you," Mum sure spends a lot of time talking about pointless draining stuff!

She is complaining about the fact that someone has moved a pair of scissors out of the man drawer and not put them back. She is always saying that she never goes anywhere near it because it's full of "Neville's useless crap." Apparently there are normally 4 pairs of scissors and she can only find one. Seriously ??

1) How come she knows they are missing if she never goes near it ?

2) Why are there 4 pairs of scissors anyway when she got rid of loads in the "minimalist" phase ?

3) Why do old people stress about stuff that totally doesn't matter ?

Unbelievable ! I came in from school, went to dance for 2 hours, came back and she is STILL on about the man drawer !!! It's like the shed conversation. I really don't want to get older if that's the sort of rubbish you end up talking about. Grandma and Grandpa are even worse - Mum says it's because retired people don't have much stress in their lives so the stupid little things become really important. Thing like worrying about how stuff is arranged in the dishwasher and making sure lights are turned off.

Grandpa told me off the other day for altering the toast setting on the toaster. He was furious and went and got the manual out and then stood in the kitchen tutting and ranting. He was shouting, "What have you done Ruby??? It was on the perfect setting, it didn't burn the bread, but it wasn't undercooked either." He reset it and then he burnt my toast. I think he did that on purpose.

Neville said it was a bit like the time him and Grandpa were arguing about the gas ignition on the BBQ and Neville was trying to tell him the best way to do it and Grandpa went ahead and lit it when Neville was still peering underneath. There was a small exploding noise, and a smell of burning hair and it turned out Neville's eyebrows nearly got completely burnt off. Grandpa wasn't very sympathetic. He just tutted and walked off saying, "You shouldn't have put your head in the way, you bloody idiot."

November 12th

There's lots of Remembrance Day stuff on the TV and there were lots of poppies in town by the war memorial. They had a service this morning but we missed it. I only saw the poppies because me and Neville popped to Sainbury's to get some extra bacon for brunch.

The Applebys made a video of the WW1 trench to show everyone the finished result. It even has little soldiers in it, doing stuff they would have done in the war, and they've put atmospheric music on the video too, it's really realistic - like a mini war film. Neville was muttering the word twat quite a lot while watching the video, but I think it looked really amazing. I hope the twins don't get any sort of award for it though, as it's so obvious they didn't make the trench… or put the video together. Neville said, "Those little shits probably spent the whole time playing Fortnite, whilst their competitive f**king parents slaved away creating that bloody masterpiece." He talks such rubbish. They are totally not old enough to play Fortnite.

Debbie's son made something similar out of a load of cereal boxes - it's not very good really, but she was very proud of it, so she put a photo of it on Facebook anyway. When you know it's supposed to be a trench you can sort of figure it out, but it wouldn't be obvious otherwise.

Neville said, "I'd love it if that twat Appleby dropped his sh*tting trench carrying it into school tomorrow."

I had loads of homework, so I spent the rest of Sunday afternoon listening to music and getting it all finished. We were just relaxing after a nice roast dinner when Mum said, "Oh No!!!! Look .... Debbie's dog has done a massive shit in her son's trench model. He's in absolute floods of tears , poor little fella."

Neville said, "I presume there's a nice close up photo of the offending turd is there?"

November 17th

Mum's gone to London to see some of her old friends. They've all gone out for a long lunch and then to some fancy cocktail bar. Margaret got the train down from up North so she could meet up with them and Suzie, Rachel, Jo and Ali are all there. For some reason Ali gets called the Turbot - I don't know why, it's not very flattering. They are always very silly when they get together, but Mum is always saying "laughter and good friends are the best therapy." I kind of know what she means. Mum said Rachel could do with a good laugh, because she just had to pay a garage a ton of money to sort her car out. It had a weird smell in it that kept getting worse and it turned out there was a dead cat in the engine. That is soooooo disgusting!! Neville said, "You need to be careful in winter because they crawl in there to keep warm - get shredded up by the fan belt if you aren't careful." Urghghhgh - that made me feel a bit ill.

They are all staying at the Turbot's house for the night so me and Neville are home by ourselves. I was bored of talking to Neville after about 5 minutes, so he suggested I invite a friend over to stay and went off to spend the whole night drinking beer and shooting things on his Xbox.

November 18th

Mum got back from the Turbot's house looking really really tired. Neville said, "Talking sh i te until the early hours were you Jaz." She said, "Well, at least I'm out socialising and talking to real people. I don't suppose you took your eyes off that bloody screen long enough to talk to another human did you ?"

Neville looked offended and said, "I had a good old chat with Ruby and Charlotte ..... didn't I Ruby?"

Well I suppose he did ... if " your pizza's ready" counts a good chat. I don't know why Mum's bothered TBH it's not like they talk to each other when they are both at home anyway.

November 19th

"I'm a celeb" started last night. I was trying to explain it to Grandpa yesterday but he just got annoyed and said, "Celebrities ??? These people aren't celebrities. I've never even heard of them - well I've heard of Harry Rednap, but that's about it. It's bloody ridiculous if you ask me. Celebrities indeed."

Shouldn't have been surprised really since there isn't anyone from Radio 4 on there ! Also it's not the same without Ant - Holly's nice I suppose, but it's just not as funny as it used to be. We were all talking about that today and Mr Piggott kept telling us all off.

November 21st

Coco had a mufti day at school - they had to pay £1 and dress as a Disney character to raise money for a local charity. Auntie Sophie said all the girls (and several of the boys) were Princesses, mostly from Frozen. There was a picture of Coco as Elsa on the WhatsApp. Auntie Sophie said when the teacher went round collecting the mufti money Horatio gave her a £50 note because he said Mummy didn't have any change. And Ophelia missed the bus this morning, because she spent so long sorting out her princess dress, so her Dad had to bring her to school in the helicopter.

It's a bit different to the schools round here !

November 23rd

I'm going to Em's for a sleepover tonight - but she has a music performance thing so I can't go over there until about 7 o'clock. I wanted to have a bath and hair wash, but Mum has taken over the bathroom for some kind of candle-lit full moon bath ritual , whatever that is !

Neville said, "She's been rattling on about it being a full moon tonight and putting all her stupid rocks in the garden. The bath thing is some kind of meditation b*llocks."

I tried banging on the door but she just shouted, "Go away Ruby , I'm taking time to contemplate and reflect - it's very, very important before starting a new lunar cycle. I need to make myself fully centred so I can face any stresses or obstacles that lie ahead."

Brilliant. And I have to go to Em's with greasy hair !

November 24th

Sleepover last night was BRILLIANT. I washed my hair there instead - which was actually better as they have this amazing walk in rainfall shower that you can play music in as well.

We had a Chinese takeaway and watched Thursday night's "I'm a celeb" as well as last night's episode. The bush tucker trial on Thursday was horrific!! James and Nick had all these things dumped on them in this box. There were mealworms, cockroaches, scorpions and about 20 MASSIVE spiders. I HATE spiders - I've actually never liked them, but it's been worse in the last few years. When I was about 9 or 10 I used to put my knickers on the radiator in winter so they were warm and toasty in the morning getting ready for school. I was just pulling a warm pair on one morning, when there

was this weird ticklish feeling and there was actually a spider IN MY
PANTS!!

I screamed "SPIDER" and Mum came running upstairs to my room -
I'd managed to get the pants off by then and they were lying on the
floor. She thought I'd just seen the spider sitting on the pants on the
radiator and told me "not to make such a fuss about nothing." When
I explained that I hadn't known the spider was there and only
discovered it once I'd put the pants ON, she was a bit more
understanding. She doesn't mind spiders but even she shuddered a
bit and admitted having one in her knickers might be a bit much.

The ones in Australia are really, really big. There's some called
Huntsmans that are ABSOLUTELY ENORMOUS. As Neville said,
"You'd certainly know about it if one of those buggers got into your
pants!"

I should actually blame Neville for the whole incident - he was the
one that told me about "radiator pants" in winter in the first place.

I think maybe tonight's episode was even WORSE - they had to hold
creatures in their mouths for 60 seconds .. urghhghgh . Harry Rednap
(who is really old but quite funny) had to hold a whole glass of like
worm things in his mouth. OMG ! So disgusting.

November 26th

I wanted to put "I'm a celeb" on and Neville was moaning about it. He said, "It's a load of total crap, it's the same f**king thing every year, when you've seen one nobody choke down a testicle, you've seen all of them."

OH MY GOD.

Mum told him not to be so miserable and told him to "go and shoot things or whatever it is you do on that stupid Xbox thing." She said it was fine if I wanted to watch it as long as all my homework was finished. She was going out to something called a Gong Bath. She's obsessed with baths. But apparently it's not a bath with water in it.

She said, "It's a vibrational sound meditation and it soothes and detoxes the body - it's like having a massage without touch, completely relaxing and rejuvenating. It can be transformative in helping you unblock your emotions."

Well I don't know what emotions it unblocked, but she had a big row with Neville when she got home.

November 29th

So in spite of saying he never watches it, Neville informed me that on "I'm a celeb" last night, 2 of the "reality TV nobs" (what he calls them!) had to eat tons of really, really disgusting things and they kept looking like they were going to throw up. Neville said, "You'd have loved it Ruby, there were giblets." Mum said, "Don't wind her up Neville, you know she hates you talking about giblets." But Neville just said, "What Jaz? I'm not winding her up - I'm just stating facts. That bloke ate a sheep's penis."

I was just walking out of the room disgusted when he added, "Oh… and he ate a sheep's arse as well."

OMG - I am totally NOT watching that on catch up.

November 30th

Neville keeps saying he is sick of Christmas and we aren't even in December yet. Mum says she is suffering from "overwhelm" whatever that is, because lots of people are already organized, and have not only done their Christmas shopping, but wrapped everything up too.

December 1st

For once we got organised early and went and picked a tree from a Christmas Tree Farm. I think it was because she felt bad seeing all the Christmas shopping posts from everyone. The farm was packed, but it was kind of fun choosing the one we wanted and a bunch of blokes dressed like elves were cutting them down and carrying them for people. Neville insisted that he could carry the tree as he didn't want to look weak and useless in front of the elf, but he's been rubbing his back and wincing all afternoon.

We've had a fake one for the last few years so it's really nice to have a real one. We set it up and we are going to decorate it tomorrow. The only problem is you have to put water in the bowl underneath to keep it alive and the dog keeps sneaking under there and drinking all the water. We have to remember to top it up or it will be all brown in a week.

December 2nd

We had a really lovely Sunday decorating the tree. We put Christmas songs on and made everywhere look really lovely. Mum made a really nice lunch and then later on we all snuggled on the sofa and watched The Holiday. I love Jack Black in that film and the parts where the guy playing Graham cries - it's so cute. And the old man is adorable !! Me and Mum cried. We both do that when we watch films. Neville just tuts at us.

Neville says that there are big riots in France and people are setting fire to things to protest about taxes. It sounds a bit like Les Miserables but in modern times - and with hi-vis jackets. It's called "Gilet Jaune" which means 'Yellow Vest Movement'. Neville keeps saying that the French have got it right and that we should be protesting about Brexit by "burning shit". Mum told him not to be so ridiculous. Also, it would be a nightmare with the dog if EVERYONE was going around wearing hi-vis jackets - it's bad enough when the bin men turn up - she goes absolutely crazy.

She also does that with old people too - Neville is always saying, "She's just like me, she can't stand bloody pensioners."

December 3rd

We watched The Christmas Chronicles tonight - it's such a cute film ! I like that you can find anything you want on Netflix. Neville is still being like the Grinch and moaning about anyone that's being Christmassy. Miserable git ! He came home from work with a load of Christmas paper that he got cheap in Tescos. But Mum said, "We aren't using all that shiny, glittery stuff Neville - did you know none of it is recyclable? It's a complete drain on the planet. I'm surprised Ollie didn't tell you that. I've got brown paper upstairs to use."

December 5th

Jasmine has put pictures of all her beautifully wrapped Christmas gifts on Instagram and Pinterest. They look TOTALLY amazing.

239

They are all fully recyclable in really good quality brown paper and decorated with all sorts of stunning raffia, white paper that looks like lace, and little sprigs of holly and fern. There are pictures of huge numbers of presents piled in front a perfectly co - ordinated tree. Everything on the tree is white with just a hint of silver here and there. It totally looks like something out of a magazine. Ours is all different colours. I liked it when we did it but it looks a bit chavy now, next to Jasmine's one. I won't tell Mum that though.

Mum has been trying to wrap up her presents. I don't think the brown paper she got is as posh as the stuff Jasmine used, 'cos some of the parcels have ripped in places and the recyclable stuff she's used as ribbon just looks really sad.

Neville said, "They aren't very pretty are they Jaz ? Most of them look like they've been booted around the back of the post office van for a few days."

THAT was NOT the right thing to say. She burst into tears and said, "I'm just trying to do my bit for the planet and explore my creativity Neville, why can't you be supportive for once." Then she ran off upstairs and slammed the bedroom door.

Neville turned to me and said, "B*starding menopause." TBH he really is NOT sympathetic to Mum's feelings AT ALL. No wonder she gets fed up with him.

December 6th

India is getting an iPhoneXR - they cost loads. Unbelievable. Mum said it's probably because her parents are going through a "messy divorce" and they are trying to compensate by spoiling her with expensive presents.

Mum said, "I'm sure you'd rather come from a happy home than have expensive gadgets like that." Yeah right !

Apparently India's dad was having an affair with a woman at his golf club who is "a bit unstable" according to a conversation I heard last night between Mum and Neville. Neville was saying, "Unstable Jaz? Unstable? Martin works with her, she's a deranged bloody psychopath."

Mum said, "You can't say things like that Neville, it's offensive to people with mental health issues."

But he just said, "I can say it if it's true."

December 8th

Mum is fuming about Jasmine (again!). Her husband got her a little "pre-Christmas" Christmas gift. It was silk pjs from The White

Company - I don't know what that shop even is, but apparently they were £189 - Woah !! That's A LOT for pjs. I don't know if it's even about the pjs TBH and think it's more that it's not even Jasmine's proper Christmas gift and it's waaaaay nicer than anything Neville has EVER got Mum.

Chloe is just soooooo spoilt ! Bridget told Mum that her daughter is in a Secret Santa group with Chloe and some of that lot and their present limit is £80 - Seriously £80 !!!!! Our group it's like £10! Neville said, " Eighty quid ??? Who are these people Ruby ?   I don't even spend that much on your Mother."

And Mum said, "Unfortunately Ruby that is absolutely true."

December 11th

This time last year it was snowing and people were having fun - this year everyone is going on about Brexit and that fact the Prime Minister might be kicked out. I feel a bit sorry for her as everyone hates her. Mind you she looks like someone that could have played a villain in one of the Harry Potter films - she's quite scary.

Neville keeps saying, "As long as that self-serving w***er Boris doesn't get in or worse still Rees-Mogg - the spoilt rich twat."

Auntie Sophie sent a photo of Coco and Felix in these really , really cute reindeer pjs . Mum says there are loads of families doing matching Christmas pjs - parents as well. I think it's quite cute.

The Appleby's are so extra though. They have had special personalised ones printed ! So, in between the holly, and Christmas puddings and reindeers, there are little red smiley Appleby apples. There is a picture of all of them in front of their incredibly massive tree in their matching outfits trying to look like it's lots of fun. Mr Appleby looks sooooo uncomfortable. Neville says it's the most awkward family photo he's ever seen. He said, "I'd love to send that to his law firm and get someone to print copies and stick them all round the office."

Mrs Appleby is managing to do THE most inventive things ever with Elf on the Shelf and posting all the pictures on Facebook. It must be taking HOURS of her time. It must be SO hard to keep coming up with good ideas, especially for 2 elves, as the twins HAD to have one each.

Mum said she's just glad the "Elf" wasn't a thing when I was younger. Neville googled "funny elf on the shelf photos" and found a whole selection of really horrible ideas, with things like murder scenes and pole dancing, elves drinking and smoking, or vomiting and pooing in the sink. He said, "Is it wrong that my favourite is the one where a GI Joe doll is water boarding the elf?"

I thought water boarding must be a bit like paddle boarding but it totally isn't. Neville explained it. OMG human beings do horrible things to one another.

December 12th

The Prime Minister survived the vote to kick her out. I don't know if this is good or bad. Neville says it doesn't make too much difference really considering Brexit is still an absolute "shit show".

Then he said, "Talking of shit shows Jaz, Ellie called to ask if there was anything we wanted for Christmas . .. what's the f**king point ? She never buys anything anyone actually wants. She'll still end up getting us a blanket knitted out of hemp by a disabled refugee or buying a f***king goat for a village in Guatamala."

I said I might ask her for some Primark vouchers and see what happens and Neville said, "Well they CLAIM they don't use child labour in their factories so you never know your luck, she might be willing to give them some of her money."

Then he added, "How about you Jaz? Anything you'd like ? I was thinking, now that Greggs have started doing gift cards, that's your Christmas pressie sorted." Then he laughed his head off.

Mum said, "The day you get me something from Greggs as a gift is the day I present you with divorce papers."

Then he replied, "I'll remember that for future reference, if you come home one day and there's a big pile of pasties in the kitchen, then you can crack on with the lawyers, we won't even need to bother talking about it."

Mum shouted back, "And you'll find the complete box set of every single episode of Downton Abbey as your clue that I'm throwing you out."

Honestly it's pathetic - especially after she's been banging on about "honest communication being the thing that deepens a relationship" again this week.

December 13th

Mum and her friends are having a "Christmas Do" at Jane's house. They are doing Secret Santa. Mum wouldn't show me what she bought to take along - that means it's rude and probably has something to do with giblets. Why do adults carry on like kids ? It's so sad.

There was a big bag of snacks in the cupboard that I thought were for us, but she must have taken them to Jane's house because when I went to get some before I went to bed they weren't there. So annoying. She'll be on about dieting again tomorrow !

December 14th

Mum was still in bed when I went to school - so it must have been a late one. I texted Neville and he said she came home at 3am and couldn't work out how to get the key in the door so he had to get up and let her in. He wasn't happy AT ALL because he has to get up about 6am ! He also wasn't happy because they were doing a "Christmas Jumper" day at work. He was telling me about it last night and just kept ranting, "They keep saying it's a bit a fun. It's not my idea of f**king fun. What's fun about looking like a proper bellend? And it's too hot to wear a bloody Christmas jumper. I don't know who's in charge of wasting all the profits on heating bills but the place is like a sauna. Honestly Ruby don't end up working in an office . .. it really is shit."

He was even more annoyed when he got home, as he said he's got his work Christmas party tomorrow night. It was supposed to just be a few drinks down the pub but "the same twats that thought Christmas jumpers were fun" decided it would be a "right laugh" if they all did karaoke instead.

Mum thinks it's totally hilarious - she knows Neville enjoys karaoke about as much as he enjoys watching period dramas on TV.

December 16th

Neville was at his Christmas thing last night and I was at Em's house for our Secret Santa sleepover (which was brilliant).

Mum came and picked me up - I'm guessing something went on with Neville last night as she was in a pretty bad mood. I asked Neville what had happened and he said he'd had to ring Mum really late to come and get him because the taxi company wouldn't take him home. It was partly because he was blind drunk and they thought he might be sick in the cab and partly because he was swearing at the cab driver too much. He told Mum there was no way he was doing any "b*stard karaoke without getting totally bladdered first." He also said, "And the "sh*tting taxi driver wouldn't let me take my kebab in with me." If it's anything like the ones they sell in town I'm not surprised - they smell disgusting. Worse than some of Felix's nappies.

I told Neville that and he said, "To be honest Ruby, I could've done with a nappy myself after eating it…. I've been sh*tting through the eye of a needle since about 4 o'clock this morning."

OMG.

December 18th

Neville's just shouted, "What's all this shit in the guest room Jaz ?" There's a little rug in the corner of the room, with embroidered cushions, a weird orange lamp thing and some candles, incense and all her useless boxes of moon cards or whatever they are. There's also a kind of wooden buddha in the middle and some weird pictures on the wall.

Mum came up and started arguing with him about it.

- M: It's a sacred corner I've created. It's a mental, emotional and energetic space to meditate and reflect . The Him a layan salt lamp has positive health benefits

- N: It's a load of random shit dumped in a corner more like. It looks a right bloody mess

- M: No it doesn't - they are meaningful items that put me in the right head space to connect with the divine

- N: Never mind the divine ... what about the f**king dog ? You can't leave that stuff all over the floor - she'll think that buddha thing is a bit of a tree stump to chew .

I put my headphones in right after Mum said, "Well if you could bloody well stop playing Clash of Clans long enough to sort the shed out for me, I wouldn't have to make do with a bloody corner of the spare room, now would I?"

Neville really is SO irritating. Maybe I will get a box set of Downton Abbey to put in the kitchen one day, so he thinks he's being dumped !

December 21st

Chilled out all day today before getting ready to go to a cool Christmas party. Mum says that her whole life from now on will involve staying in on a Friday night, without a drink, just so she can "provide a full time taxi service" for me. I don't know what she's on about. Surely it's her job to run me around when I need to go somewhere? Honestly parents ... always moaning on about something.

They announced the Christmas No.1 today on the Scott Mills show on Radio 1 - I thought it would be Arianna Grande or the "Sweet but Psycho" song but this really silly song about sausage rolls is No.1 - it's by a YouTuber and it's for Charity which is very cool.

Neville said, "This country's been a f**king embarrassment lately, but I'm bloody proud that a song about sausage rolls is the Number 1 Christmas record. Gives me faith in human nature."

Mum said, "It's actually fantastic - it's raised a huge amount of money for a charity that provides food banks throughout the country. Mind you we shouldn't even need food banks in a 1st world country like ours, frankly it's an utter disgrace."

Neville replied, "I don't know about that Jaz, what I DO know is that changing the lyrics from "We built this city on Rock and Roll" to "We built this City on Sausage Rolls" is compete f**king genius. I tell you something, when Chemical Banana get signed to a label and we start doing all our own stuff, instead of covers, that guy is the sort of f**king legend we need as part of our band."

I wanted to point out he's been a YouTuber for ages and he just got a number 1 record, so I'm not sure he'll need the likes of Chemical

Banana to help his career. I didn't though - it seemed a bit mean towards Neville. It is Christmas after all.

OMG - I just realised what Neville just said. Does he seriously think ANYONE will give Chemical Banana a record deal? SAD.

December 22nd

OMG Jake Lakson actually smiled at me across the room at the party yesterday. I totally thought he was smiling at someone behind me, but when I turned round there was only the snacks table behind me - no people. He smiled again when I turned back confused (he must have thought it was funny that I didn't think he was looking at me). I didn't really know what to do so I probably just looked really gormless (a bit like the dog!) Soooooo embarrassing.

I tried to tell Izzy straight after it happened, but she was too busy taking a selfie and trying to get Connor's attention.

I am still in total SHOCK. I've been boring Izzy and Em about it ALL DAY. Izzy seemed a bit put out that FOR ONCE we weren't talking about her and Dan, her and Connor or her and Rob, even though that's what we do ALL THE TIME. Typical. She's a bit of a rubbish friend when I think about it.

December 23rd

My journal has just about run out so I can't write anything else for now. I am hoping that I get a new one for Christmas. I put it on my list so hopefully Mum will ACTUALLY take notice.... turned out it was a pretty good present after all.

Here is my list:

THINGS I WANT FOR CHRISTMAS

- iphoneX or XR (seriously unlikely)
- New journal
- VERY good mascara
- Top Shop skinny jeans
- Hollister hoodie
- People to shut up about Brexit (seriously unlikely)
- Mum and Neville to shut up about the shed (even more unlikely)
- Chemical Banana to break up (about as likely as them getting a record deal)
- Less annoying parents!!!! (absolutely no chance !!)

THINGS I REALLY, REALLY WANT FOR CHRISTMAS

- Jake Lakson to smile at me again!!!!

acknowledgments

I would like to thank my daughter and husband who both helped with funny ideas for this book.

I would also like to thank friends and family members who provided creative inspiration for the characters.

Many of the characters in this book are loosely based on real people, consent has been obtained from them, although the names have been changed to protect the guilty.

Other characters are pure invention, but are inspired by the sorts of "stereotypes" you come across every day on social media.

Email: kaycarltonauthor@gmail.com

Printed in Great Britain
by Amazon

34454803R00151